ADVENTURE AT BRACKENDALE

ADVENTURE AT BRACKENDALE

by

LINDA PETERS

THE CHILDREN'S PRESS
LONDON AND GLASGOW

This Impression 1968

PRINTED AND MADE IN GREAT BRITAIN BY
WM. COLLINS SONS AND CO. LTD.
LONDON AND GLASGOW

CONTENTS

CHAPTER I

MOUNTAIN RESCUE

EVEN AS Avril drifted cosily from sleep to wakefulness she had an uneasy feeling of something not quite right. It was the absence of real noise. There was none of the usual clatter of lorries and cars passing in the street below. The sounds she heard were strange: the music of a stream as it gurgled happily over stones; the lowing of cattle, and the distant baa-ing of sheep. For a moment she lay and wondered where she was.

Above her was a white-painted ceiling, across which went thick wooden beams. The sun was streaming through a half-opened window, and as the French girl raised herself on one elbow, memory came flooding back. She shot a swift glance at the other bed, and seeing it was empty she swept back the bedclothes, grabbed her deep-red dressing-gown and tiptoed to the window.

Kneeling, she looked out over a farmyard. Sheep were milling in a paddock and an oldish man was coaxing a score of them, aided by a shaggy dog, towards a pen. Beyond the farmyard she could see several fields, and farther still a bracken-covered valley which ended in beetling hills lit up by sunshine.

Beyond the hilltops the sky was a soft blue across which cotton-wool clouds drifted slowly.

"So, Avril Leresche," she murmured, drawing in a deep breath of the pleasantly scented air. "So this is Brackendale Farm by daylight. How lovely—and last night, when my pen-friend Ann was sleeping, and all was so very quiet, I was silly enough to be just a little homesick for Paris." She closed her eyes for a moment, remembering the long hour she had spent staring at the blue-black rectangle of uncurtained window. She had felt sad, then. Stars seen through the window had winked like minute diamonds. The stream's babble had possessed a mysterious, almost frightening music. Far away, just as it had seemed she might drop off to sleep, an owl had called. The sound had sent goose-flesh creeping up her cheeks. It was all so very different from Paris. In that farmhouse bedroom there had been no clatter and roar of distant traffic.

"Avril . . . hallo, come on, sleepy-head. There's coffee in the kitchen."

Avril opened her eyes, then waved to the girl who had just come from the cowshed. She carried a jug of milk in each hand, straight from the cooler, and seen from above, the sun made her flaxen hair look almost silvery. Ann Birkett set down her jugs and made motions of washing her face, then picking up her milk once more strode towards the farmhouse.

Avril smiled and shook her head as Ann disappeared from sight.

"Is not her father the farmer?" she murmured. "Yet she works like a labourer. And such clothes, too . . . breeches and heavy boots like a man!"

She turned from the window and slipped her arms into the sleeves of her silk dressing-gown. A few moments later the door of the bedroom opened and Ann, all smiles, came in.

"Did you sleep well? I hope you did. Y'know, sometimes people find it hard to drop off the first night . . . especially people who live in towns. The quietness seems to. . . ."

"I *did* sleep," Avril interrupted, looking in bewilderment again at the whipcord breeches, the thick stockings, and the checked cotton shirt her friend wore. For the moment she had discarded her climbing-cum-farm boots and was now wearing slippers.

"Oh, yes, you were sleeping sound enough when I got up. Anyway . . . I'll fetch you some hot water and coffee. I won't be more than two shakes of a lamb's tail."

She was as good as her word, and within a minute or so was back with a large enamel jug of hot water and a small jug of coffee which smelled delicious. The cup was hooked on to her little finger.

"You know it *would* just happen when you came," she explained. "As I told you last night, Mummy has had to go away. My aunt has had a slight accident, and as she lives alone, someone has to stay with her for a few days. I hope you won't mind?"

"Non . . . non," then Avril spread her hands in a

gesture as she said: "I am sorry . . . it is agreed that
I speak only English, yes? So . . . I begin again. You
ask if I mind your mother not being here for a few
days. I do not mind! I shall be glad to help you. I
shall learn much!"

"It means I shan't be quite as free to take you sight-
seeing," Ann explained, pouring coffee. "We have
two visitors in . . . we take paying guests, you know.
People who come here for a holiday. Our present guests
are two ladies . . . schoolteachers. So, of course, I
must cook breakfast for them, make up lunches, and
cook an evening meal. But it will only be for a day
or so."

"It will be fun," Avril insisted, sipping her coffee
and nodding approval. "I shall have a quick wash, then
join you. You know something . . .?"

"What?"

"Last night, when I come here in the dark . . . I am
tired, and a little voice inside me keeps saying: ' How
nice if you had never come. You will not like this
place in the hills. It is dark, and lonely, and even the
light is from an oil lamp.' No . . . no . . ." she went on
hurriedly, as she laid a reassuring hand on Ann's arm.
"This morning I am so very glad that I have come.
Everything is beautiful. The hills, the sky, the sheep
. . . even the old man and his dog."

"Oh, you'll like Thomas," Ann assured her. "He's
a pet. D'you know, I think he knows every stone, piece
of bracken and blade of grass round here. He's . . .
hallo, that sounds like a horse."

She hurried over to the open window and leaned out.

"It is a horse," she said a few moments later, turning to face her friend. "It looks like Mervin Rigg from the village. Will you excuse me a moment? There must be something wrong."

As Ann hurried from the spotlessly clean bedroom, Avril finished off her coffee. Then pouring the steaming water into the old-fashioned wash-bowl, she picked up the cake of soap. Looking at it she smiled, for Ann Birkett had remembered her French friend's favourite brand, and it made Avril realise that even in small things no pains had been spared to make her happy from the very start of her holiday.

She had just finished dressing when there was a knock on the bedroom door, and a moment later Ann was in and saying a little breathlessly:

"Everything happens at once, Avril. It *was* Mervin Rigg, with news that a plane for Prestwick made a crash landing over the top of the fell last night. One of the crew got down to a village on the other side and police telephoned through to see if the people from this valley could get up there to help."

"And this Mr. Rigg . . . he has come to ask your father to help?" Avril asked.

"Yes, he and Thomas. They'll be away in a few minutes. I'm sorry about . . . "

"But it is not your fault," Avril broke in. "Perhaps we could help, yes?"

"Well, in a way, yes!" Ann agreed. "Father and Thomas were going to bring the second batch of sheep off the fells to-day, for dipping. I promised I would see to that. I hope you don't mind. You could rest, and . . ."

"But, no!" Avril broke in, and her eyes were bright with excitement. "I shall help, too. Please do not think that because I live in Paris I cannot climb mountains. I have brought my boots. Come . . . I am excited. Let us see the rescue people start."

They hurried quietly down the stairs, past the two bedrooms where the schoolteacher guests were either still sleeping, or dressing, and so out into the farm-yard. Ann's father joined them in a few moments. He had a rucksack, on the back of which was strapped a light metal framework. It was part of a collapsible stretcher. Old Thomas joined his master a minute or so later, carrying a similar rucksack. Elderly though he was, Thomas was a valued member of the mountain rescue team because of his knowledge of the hills in all kinds of weather.

"This is Miss Leresche, Thomas," Ann's father said. "She comes from Paris."

"Good morning, Miss," Thomas said, touching his cap. He was a man in his sixties, with a face seamed and wrinkled like old leather; but there was an impish twinkle in his faded blue eyes as he went on: "I wonder if you know an old feller called Pierre Mott? I met him during the 1914-18 war, and he came from Paris. He'd a little blue scar on his chin. I dessay you'll have seen him many a time, eh?"

Avril blinked, looked quickly at Ann, then said a little breathlessly:

"But . . . m'sieur . . . Paris is . . . it is a city. A big city."

"O—oh!" Thomas scratched at his silvering hair as if perplexed. "I always thought Paris was . . . well, y'know, just a village."

"M'sieur!"

"Don't take any notice of him, Avril," Ann said laughing. "He's just pulling your leg. He knows Paris isn't a village. He was in hospital in Paris . . . oh, before we were born."

"I think we'd better be going, boss," Thomas chuckled, swinging his laden rucksack on to his back. "I have a feeling Miss Avril belongs to the Fighting French, and . . ."

"No, no, no," Avril was smiling again. "Do not be alarmed, m'sieur Thomas . . . I am never angry with *very* old men. They forget so easily, yes?"

Thomas grinned and thrust out his right hand.

"I think we're going to like one another, Miss Leresche. I'm right glad to meet you, and I hope you enjoy every minute of your holiday here. If Ann gets too tired to take you on the fells, just come for me. We'll . . ."

"Come on, Thomas," Ann's father interrupted. "This isn't the time for chit-chat. Take your time with the sheep, Ann. It doesn't matter if you can't manage to get them all down. And don't forget our visitors."

A hand wave to Avril and the two men were on

their way, moving with the steady, mile-eating pace
of fell men. Ann stood for a moment, watching, then
turned back to the house.

Both girls were far too busy for the next hour to
have time to think of anything but the comfort of
their two guests. Miss Pringle and Miss Armstrong
were both interested in Avril, and at first had the idea
that she had come to the farm as a maid for the holiday
season.

When breakfast was over and packed lunches had
been put up for the two visitors Avril looked at Ann,
a little smile on her face.

"I think I would like the Miss Armstrong as a
teacher," she said. "She is very nice, and quiet, yes?
But . . . la—la, Miss Pringle! So tall and strong, like
a man almost. And the voice. She talks like an angry
gendarme . . . er . . . policeman, eh? I would not like
to offend her. I think she would frighten all her
pupils into working very hard."

"I imagine it is just her manner," Ann suggested,
beginning to wash the breakfast crockery. "Sit down,
Avril. It won't take me long to finish these."

"I am not a paying guest," the French girl protested,
taking up the cloth and beginning to dry the cups.
"I am a friend . . . so, we keep together. If you do work
about the house . . . then I do work about the house."

"But you are on holiday," Ann insisted.

"So . . . a holiday is doing something different,"
Avril laughed. "I enjoy this. Afterwards, we go for
the sheep."

They left the house only when they had dusted and made the beds. Then, each wearing boots, and with the two sheep-dogs at their heels, they started for the fells. The sheep in the paddock were contentedly cropping the grass. A lark was singing its heart out somewhere in the blue sky, and the dew was already sucked up by the summer sun.

There was only a faint track up the valley, and they crossed and re-crossed the stream a number of times. They finally left the grass and went through patches of bracken almost a yard high, then came out on to rocks. They scrambled up these and came on to the ridge which connected two high fells. From there they could look across to the spot where the plane had come down during the night.

"I would like to go, but I am frightened," Avril said, watching a helicopter, looking like a giant dragonfly, as it whirred away from the spot. "I hope no one was killed or badly injured."

"We'll know later, when Dad returns," Ann said, "and in a day or so we'll go over and look at the crash. There's one thing, the pilot was lucky, for he's come down at about the only place where it is reasonably smooth."

She had sent the two dogs off to round up the black-faced sheep which were grazing on the thin, wiry grass, and soon they could see little grey blobs beginning to move down into the long valley. Avril was amazed at the number of Herdwick sheep being gathered together.

"I see only one or two," she confessed. "Where have they all come from? They have been hiding? Perhaps they know they must come down to the farm to be dipped."

"I don't think so," Ann chuckled. "They're so much the colour of the rocks that you could walk quite close to one and if it did not move you might not see it."

The dogs ran here and there, rounding up odd sheep from craggy places where it seemed there could not be even a blade of grass. Then, with one dog moving silently behind the main flock, they started for the farm. Only then did the second dog break the quietness of the sun-heated rocks.

His sharp, commanding yapping made Ann stop and turn. Even Avril sensed something wrong.

"I hope he hasn't found a dead ewe," Ann said. "You stay here if you like, Avril. It isn't too easy across there."

"No, no, no," Avril protested. "Ann . . . I climb in the French Alps, you know; just for pleasure, of course; but I climb. Please . . . may I come?"

"Of course; I was only thinking it will be warm work."

They began to climb a rock-strewn slope, and after only one more sharp, shrill, yapping bark, the dog was silent. She knew they were coming, and that barking would not bring them to her any quicker.

Nell, the sheep-dog, wagged her tail as they drew near, then seemed to poke her long nose into the rocks.

When she looked up again her tail was wagging furiously as if she was trying to say:

"Come and look here, and then you'll see what a clever dog I am."

When they reached the spot both girls were amazed to see a yard-wide fissure in the ground, and faintly discernible at a depth of about fifteen feet was a frightened ewe. As if aware that help was at hand the ewe looked up and bleated appealingly.

"But this is dangerous," Avril said. "Suppose a man or woman walked this way. Pouf . . . and they disappear. Should there not be a notice . . . to say 'Keep away'?"

Ann nodded absentmindedly and stared down the crevice for a moment or so. Then, suddenly looking round, she said:

"I'm sorry, Avril. What did you say?"

"I think there should be a notice . . ."

"Oh, yes, yes," Ann agreed, then with a little shrug, "Of course there aren't an awful lot of people come round here. They usually keep to the tracks. I don't suppose anybody has seen this before. A crevice like this might only have opened up during the winter." While she was speaking she was beginning to unwind the rope she had carried over her shoulder.

"You will go down?" Avril asked.

"I wouldn't . . . if the ewe could fasten the rope round herself," Ann said, laughing softly. "Anyway, there isn't any particular danger. I don't suppose you'd get more th. n a nasty shaking if you fell to the bottom.

The rocks are very smooth, and there seems to be earth to fall on. Will you hold the end of the rope while I see if it will reach?"

With Avril holding one end Ann tossed the free end down, and it fell gently over the ewe, making her yellow eyes blink in surprise. There seemed to be a few feet to spare.

"Now," Ann murmured, looking round, "if we can . . . ah, just the thing. Look, Avril, we'll fasten one end round this knob of rock . . . it might have been made for us. Then I'll climb down, fasten the free end round the ewe, climb up again, and then we'll haul her ladyship back to safety."

They fastened their end of the rope round the finger of rock, and tested it for strength. As Ann had said, the rock might have been specially carved out by wind and rain specially for this work. It was a foot high and shaped roughly like an eye-tooth.

"You just see that it doesn't slip over the top," Ann counselled, "and we're all right."

Avril nodded. She had climbed with a party of French teenagers in the Alps, and knew a little about rock climbing. The climb down to the trapped ewe was not a dangerous proposition.

Easing herself over the edge of the crevice, while Nell sniffed anxiously as if surprised that her mistress should be doing such a thing, Ann began the descent.

Below her the ewe had backed into a niche in the rock, as if afraid that something might fall on her. Gripping the rope tightly, Ann eased herself down, trying to get one nailed boot against the smooth rock face to steady her swinging. She could not do it, for the crevice widened a few feet below ground, and she just dangled on the rope.

She was only a matter of three feet from the crevice floor when she thought she heard a startled cry from above. Checking her descent she looked up, shouting:

"Hallo . . . hallo! Avril! AVRIL!"

There was a tiny little jerk on the rope, almost as if someone was trying to haul her up, then the rope slipped an inch or so, halted, and in that instant, sensing trouble, Ann took a quick look down and began to slide for the bottom.

Her feet were less than a foot from the soft earth when the rope ceased to be taut in her hands. She dropped, her boots sank easily into a pile of soft earth, and as she rolled over, the rope came slithering down on top of her while the startled ewe bleated in fear and astonishment.

Scrambling to her knees, and then to her feet, Ann looked up. Nell was there, now barking furiously. Then she disappeared and Ann waited for Avril to look down. Instead it was Nell again, barking and barking, her eyes wild with excitement.

"Avril . . . Avril . . . AVRIL!" Ann's heart was thumping from the shock of the fall, and the sudden dropping around her of the rope. She was quite unhurt, but shaken out of her usual calm.

Nell disappeared once more, and re-appeared, still barking furiously. Ann cupped her hands about her mouth and shouted again as loud and as shrilly as she could:

"AV——REEL . . . AAAAV . . . REEEL!"

There was no reply. She thought she could hear the faint barking of Nell, the sheep-dog, then even that sound ceased.

CHAPTER II

THE MYSTERIOUS RESCUER

FOR A FEW moments Ann panicked. She knew enough about rocks and climbing to realise that only by a miracle could she climb unaided out of this crevice. The rocks were too smooth to give finger or footholds; but the thing which frightened her first of all was why the rope had come down. A wild, lunatic thought crossed her mind for a moment that Avril had deliberately slipped the loop off the rock.

"Idiot," she told herself, "she couldn't have done it . . . not with your weight on the rope. The rock snapped off. That's what it did, I'm sure."

The thought gave her a little comfort until she asked herself why Avril had not come to the mouth of the crevice. And what had happened to Nell? Surely her own sheep-dog had not deserted her.

Even as those thoughts were going through her mind Nell reappeared. She looked down, stretched a paw as if contemplating trying to reach Ann, then drew it back and whined.

"Fetch her, Nell," Ann called up. "Fetch her, there's a good girl. Fetch . . . fetch . . . fetch."

Whining softly, as if to say she did not quite know

what to do for the best, Nell moved out of sight and for several anxious minutes there was a period of complete silence. It was broken when Nell began barking once more.

A few moments later the dog poked her head over the crevice lip, and a second later the head of Avril was also shutting out some of the sunlight. The two girls looked at one another in silence for a second, then both began:

"Are you hurt?" There followed a short pause as each waited for the other to answer. Then, as if worked by clockwork, they both said together: "No . . . I'm all right," and stopped again. It was Avril who spoke next:

"Please, Ann . . . you speak first."

"I'm not hurt! What's the matter with you? Is it the light, or . . . you look pale. Are you hurt?"

"I'm getting better quickly," Avril said. " Oh, Ann, what idiots we are, eh? We say we have climbed mountains, and we tie the rope round a rock which has a crack in it. I hear it begin to break. I make a snatch at the rope; but I am too late. The rock broke and I am jerked off my feet. I fall across a stone and . . . poooof! All the air is gone from me. I am like a fish out of water. I gasp and pant . . . I am like a dog that has been running for a long time, so . . ." and she gave an imitation of gasping for breath.

"But you are not hurt?"

"Only my pride is wounded deep," Avril agreed. "But you, Ann; if you are not hurt then we must get you out quickly. Please, throw up the rope. Then I shall haul you up, yes?"

Ann coiled the rope and tried to throw it up to her friend. The loops spread out as they went upwards, but just failed to get within reach of Avril's hand.

"That is very good try," the French girl encouraged. "Next time . . . and I have it easily."

The next time, however, the rope did not reach quite as far, and from then on for ten minutes, until Ann's arm and shoulders were aching, the rope was tossed upwards again and again. Each time it either struck the rocks and tumbled down, or sailed lazily to within a foot of Avril's fingers, then faltered and fell back again.

"Stop, stop, stop!" Avril finally commanded. "We can play like this all the day. Rest, and I shall come down a little. It should not be difficult. If I come down a metre . . . then all is settled. The rope will be in my hands at once."

"I don't know," Ann shook her head doubtfully. "The rock sides are so smooth. One slip and you . . ."

"I shall *not* slip," Avril interrupted cheerfully. "It is the French way to take a risk for the big prize. Can we stay here all day? No, of course not. So . . . coil the rope, and I shall come down a little way towards you."

"Be very careful," Ann pleaded, then watched in silence as her friend eased herself over the lip of the crevice and began to feel with her booted feet for a foothold.

Even Nell seemed to sense that this was a moment for silence, for she ceased her soft whimperings and stared at Avril as the French girl lowered herself cautiously into the crevice, her back braced against one rock wall, her feet against the other. Ann's heart missed a beat as there was a sudden scraping of nails on the rock, and Avril's right foot swung into space. A few moments later, however, she was in position, wedged tightly across the crevice ready for Ann's next rope-throwing attempt.

The coil swung upwards, and went cleanly over the taut legs.

"There, *ma cherie*," Avril chanted, "I ought to have done this first of all, then we should both have been out in the sunshine by now. You will have to write me a letter saying what a brave mountaineer I am, eh? Avril Leresche so brave; so clever; so strong. She . . ." While she had been talking she had been knotting the end of the rope about her right arm. Then she started trying to wriggle upwards. It was at that moment she ceased her light-hearted chatter. She did not wriggle upwards. . . but lost an inch or so, her body slipped downwards while her feet remained in the same spot on the opposite wall of rock.

The "chimney" technique in climbing has been used by mountaineers for a long time. With the back braced against one wall of rock and the feet against the other, climbers have ascended vertical "chimneys" which would have been impossible to climb by any other method. For some reason, however, Avril was making progress in the wrong direction.

At the end of five minutes she paused to rest, conscious that her leg muscles were tiring. Yet if she did not keep her feet jammed against the opposite wall of rock, she would drop like a stone the twelve feet down to Ann. If that happened they were indeed trapped. Only Nell knew where they were, and the sheep-dog watched from the top. She was whining again, now, as if conscious that something had gone wrong with the French girl's plan.

"It is my coat which keeps holding," Avril said. "I think maybe the belt is caught on something. I shall try again . . . in a moment."

She did try again, but without gaining an inch. Ann watched in anxious silence. Twelve feet of a drop, even though Avril would alight on a pile of peaty soil, could be disastrous. Yet she kept her fears to herself, and could not but admire Avril's courage as she struggled again and again to work herself up to the crevice top.

Finally, as if deciding that she would never manage the climb, Avril called out.

"I am sorry, Ann, but I think I shall have to join you. My legs are so stiff and aching . . . they must soon betray me. Will you please get out of the way, then I shall not hurt you when I fall. I think I cannot stay here much longer. There is a cramp coming in my muscles."

"Wait . . . wait," Ann pleaded. "I'll try and scoop as much of the earth into a pile . . . then you won't hurt yourself. If I . . . Nell! NELL! Be quiet."

The sheep-dog had suddenly begun to bark furiously, and in the confines of the crevice the sound was thunderous, drowning speech completely.

"I shall count ten," Avril shouted, trying hard to keep down the rising tide of panic which was beginning to make her heart thump madly. "Then I must fall. My legs will not hold me."

On hands and knees below, Ann Birkett scrabbled at the earth, softening it still more and heaping it directly beneath her friend. Above, Nell had stopped barking. Avril had closed her eyes. Her lips were compressed into a thin line as she fought against the growing pain in her leg muscles and the fear which was flooding over her.

Then, in the grim silence which enveloped that mountain crevice a man's voice said:

"Here, grab this. Come on . . . quick, before you fall."

Ann paused in her scraping-up of earth, hardly daring to believe what she heard. Avril opened her eyes, blinked, then cautiously drew one hand away from the rock at her back and gripped the sleeve of a coat. The movement caused one foot to slip. Avril made a wild grab with her other hand at the sleeve, and that broke her rigid position. One foot slid down, then the other, and a moment later she was dangling in space.

She dropped several inches, her grip on the coat sleeve tightening spasmodically.

"Easy, now, don't panic," the man's voice urged, even though stitches in the coat were beginning to crack under the strain.

Below, still kneeling, Ann Birkett looked up and hardly dared breathe. She saw Avril start to spin slowly round. Above her she could see a coat, but with no sign of the person who held it. Then came instructions from the unseen man. In a calm, matter of fact voice, he told Avril what to do: to get her feet against the rock, to pull herself into a sitting position, then "walk" up the rocky wall as the man hauled on the coat.

It was all over in two minutes. The light shone down clear on to Ann, with Avril out in the open again. Then the head and shoulders of the rescuer appeared. He was smiling, and he waved a hand.

"Now, if you'll tie the rope round yourself, miss, I'll help you out."

Ann waited for the rope, then asked their rescuer if he would haul up the ewe first. He did this, hauling gently so that the frightened animal would not be hurt. Then the rope came down once more and Ann was helped out.

Avril was sitting on the wiry grass, massaging her calf muscles. She grinned ruefully and with a shrug said:

"You will please forget what I said about writing a letter saying that I am a clever mountaineer, Ann.

I think I make foolish mistake. But for this gentle-
man . . . we should be in an awkward position, eh?"

Ann nodded. She was rather breathless from her
climb, and could only stand and smile at her rescuer.
He was a man of medium height, quite slim in build,
and wearing rather shabby tweeds. She noticed, too,
that he needed a shave.

"I saw you come over here," he said, coiling the rope
with an easy skill which suggested he might well be
a mountaineer himself. "I saw one of you disappear,
then the other, and thought I'd slip across and see
what was going on."

"We're very, very much in your debt," Ann managed
to say. "Thank you . . . er . . . Mr. . . . er . . ."

"Just call me Bill," the man said, grinning. "Did
you come up here for the sheep? Do you belong here?"

"I am a visitor," Avril said, "Ann . . . she is from the
farm at the bottom of the fell—that is the right word,
Ann—fell? This English sometimes puzzles. If I drop
down a hole in the ground then I *fell* down. If I come
up the hillside . . . I come up a *fell*," and with a little
smile she shrugged again.

"You sound foreign," Bill suggested. "French?"

"I am from Paris! You know Paris?"

"I was there a few weeks ago, I am . . ." and there he
stopped, then patted his pockets and brought out a
packet of cigarettes. "Smoke? No! Hm! It's nice to
meet girls who don't smoke. In fact, *I* won't have a
smoke . . . I'm running a bit short."

"Are you walking round here?" Ann asked. "I—

we would like to repay you a little for your kindness.
I wondered if you would care to come down to the
farm and have something to eat. That is . . . if you are
making for the valley. I know my father would like
to thank you for what you did. We would have been
in a real mess if you hadn't come along."

Bill pursed his lips for a moment, changed his mind
about not having a smoke and, after tapping the butt
of the cigarette on a thumb nail, struck a match and
after drawing deeply on it asked:

"I wonder if I dare ask a favour?"

"If we can help you, yes," Ann assured him. "What
is it?"

Again there was a pause, as if Bill was weighing
something in his mind. He was a youngish man,
perhaps twenty-six, though it was hard to tell, for
when he smiled he seemed almost boyish.

"This may seem odd to you," he began slowly.
"I'm up here to do a job. I thought it would only take
me a matter of hours. I brought a good waterproof,
and some food; but it looks as if I might be here a day
or so. I was . . ."

"We have a spare room at Brackendale," Ann interrupted. "We just have two guests in . . . that is, in
addition to Avril, who is my friend. So we could . . ."
She stopped for Bill was shaking his head.

"Thanks very much . . . and by the way I don't
know *your* names." He shook hands as Ann introduced
Avril and then gave her own name. "Anyway, thanks
very much for the offer . . . but much as I'd like to

accept, I can't. The job I have to do can't be done unless I stay on the hills continually. I was wondering if you could fetch me some supplies . . . food, maybe a little pan I could boil water in to make coffee. No?" as both girls looked a little bewildered.

"Oh . . . oh, yes, we'd do that," Ann said quickly. "I'm afraid I just thought it . . . well . . ." she ended lamely.

"I know, it seems odd," Bill agreed. "It is odd. I said it was. It just happens that I have to do it. However, if it isn't convenient . . ."

"No . . . no . . . no," Avril put in anxiously. "Please, you have done so much for us. Ann, we could do what Mr. Bill asks, yes? So, there," as Ann nodded. "If you tell Ann what you want . . . then I hope we shall bring it, quickly."

"Not *so* quickly, I'm afraid," Ann countered, and in explanation went on: "You see, we're bringing down the sheep for my father. Most of the men from the valley have been called out to the plane crash . . . and our sheep are due for dipping. We'll have to get them down to the farm. So it would be late . . . might even be to-morrow. I have to cook for our two guests."

"That would do fine," Bill agreed. "Look, I'll scribble down a list of the things I'd like."

He made out a list, insisted on giving them at least twice as much money as the things would cost, and arranged to be at a spot lower down the fell the next morning to pick them up.

"And if you can't make it for morning, don't worry," he said, smiling, "I can pick up the stuff later. And thanks a lot for helping. Now I suppose you'd better be off with your sheep, eh?"

"Mister Bill," Avril said, a quizzical smile on her face. "This work . . . it is very secret, yes?"

He smiled and nodded.

"It is rather. And it's important that nobody knows about it until the job is done. Sorry I can't tell you now!"

Avril shrugged and sighed deeply.

"I love secrets," she hinted. "And we are very good at keeping secrets, aren't we, Ann?"

Bill shook his head, still smiling.

"Don't tempt me. I promise to tell you the whole secret when I've finished the job," he said. "And if you don't mention me to anyone . . . that will help enormously. Can I bank on you?"

"Oh, yes," Avril's reply was immediate. "We owe you so very much. It is so little you ask in return. We shall not say one word, eh, Ann? Not one word."

Ann smilingly agreed.

Bill gave them a wave and then started off through the bracken for the higher slopes of the fell while Ann and Avril moved across the rocks, with the watchful Nell shepherding the rescued ewe before her.

"He is good-looking," Avril said when they had walked for several minutes in silence. "I wonder what he does . . . alone, in the hills!"

"Now, Avril," Ann said, wagging a warning finger
"The best thing is to try and forget him . . . and th
secret. I think we shouldn't talk about him. In fac
we had perhaps better not mention our little acciden
If father gets to know he will want to hear all abou
it; who the man was who rescued us; and . . . he'l
certainly think it very odd if we can't tell him wher
Bill came from, or where he is staying."

Avril agreed, and they continued down the fell in
silence, each busy with her own thoughts, and th
thoughts were the same . . . Bill and his secret. Why
should a man be staying out on the fells, apparentl
not wanting anyone to know he was there?

In the valley bottom they caught up with Shep. Thei
second dog had gathered a flock of some eighty ewe
into a stone fold, and was waiting for instructions. B
the time these had been herded down to Brackendale
farm it was four o'clock. Ann counted the sheep, ther
went in to wash and snatch a quick bite and a welcom
cup of tea before milking their four cows.

At half past six the two schoolteacher guests return
ed, tired from a long tramp across the fells. The big
cooker, which also heated water, provided enough ho
water for baths, and in the kitchen Ann had been busy
with Avril helping. They put out the evening meal
and had just served the coffee when the sound of iron-
shod boots in the yard announced the return of Mr.
Birkett and Thomas.

The two men came into the kitchen, thankfully took
off their boots, washed, and sat down to a huge meal.

Ann and Avril were anxious to know all about the plane crash; but it was a rule in the Birkett house that the only conversation at meal times should be such phrases as: pass the potatoes, pass the meat, the salt, or anything else on the table.

Not until Ann had poured four cups of coffee, and Thomas had lit his old briar pipe did Mr. Birkett ask about the sheep. Ann gave him the total number brought in and he nodded.

"And you, Mr. Birkett?" Avril asked, having re-trained her curiosity with the greatest difficulty. "Was it a bad crash? Were people killed?"

"No, fortunately there was no one killed. Though I don't know how the pilot chap managed it," Mr. Birkett said, filling his own pipe. "He was mighty lucky to put the plane down on a long slope. It doesn't look too badly damaged, but I doubt if they'll ever get it into the air again. It was one of those miracles; not a soul killed. A number of people slightly injured, one or two broken bones and a lot of bruises, of course. The oddest thing . . ." He stopped and looked up, at the sound of a tap on the kitchen door.

"It's only me, Mr. Birkett," came the voice of Miss Pringle. "May I come in?"

"Yes, yes, do come in, Miss Pringle. I hope you and Miss Armstrong have had a nice day. It's been one of those days with a bit o' breeze, yet sunny."

"We've had a lovely day," Miss Pringle said, moving into the room and making space for her friend Miss Armstrong. "We were just curious to know if there was any truth in this rumour ... I suppose it's only a rumour ... about the man who is missing from the plane crash."

"They used to call it Bush Telegraph when I was in the army," Thomas chuckled. "Nobody knew who started the story, but before you could look round everybody knew."

"Then it isn't true," Miss Pringle sounded dis- appointed. "I said to Miss Armstrong that it was just a tale. Whoever heard of a fortune in precious stones being sent by plane to . . ."

"But it *is* true," Ann's father cut in. "Leastways the police are very anxious to find the fellow."

"What is this you speak of?" Avril asked, her eyes suddenly round as saucers. "A man from the plane is missing?"

"It's a queer business and no mistake!" Mr. Birkett admitted, motioning the two schoolteachers to sit down. "When this plane came down I suppose there was the usual confusion . . . maybe a bit of panic, I don't know. Anyway, the pilot and his crew got the passengers out as quick as they could . . . just in case the wreckage caught fire. Everybody was accounted for ... yet when the mountain rescue team got there— and the police, of course—a man was missing. Several people recollected seeing him; and several swore that he didn't seem to be hurt at all."

"And nobody can find him?" Avril asked, at which Ann had a sudden sick feeling that her friend was going to pour out the story of how they had met a man on

ne fell who wanted food, yet did not want anyone to
now he was up there.

"That's right, Avril," Ann's father said, "that chap
eems to have vanished into thin air. Anyway, it seems
hat he wasn't any ordinary passenger. He was a man
mployed by some big diamond dealer in London . . .
ne of these Hatton Garden people."

"So!" and Avril's eyes went even rounder. "And
his man had diamonds with him?"

"They say so," Ann's father agreed. "Seems he was
aking them up to Prestwick where he was to board
plane to take him to America. However, he's no-
vhere to be found, and the jewels—diamonds I think
he police said—have gone too."

"It seems too fantastic to be true," Miss Pringle
aid, her eyes gleaming. "I suppose he succumbed to
emptation. Did they say how much the missing
ewels . . . diamonds, were valued at?"

Thomas chuckled and taking out his pipe said:

"Well, now, if you believed half what was being
aid among the search party it were anything from
en thousand quid to the Crown Jools. You heard
omething, didn't you, boss?"

"The sergeant from Cockermouth said he had heard
the missing gems were worth about a hundred and
seventy thousand pounds," Mr. Birkett said. "Supposed
to be in a leather satchel which was fastened to the
man's wrist by a steel chain. Whether he had a key
or not nobody seemed to know."

"I suppose there'll be a reward for their recovery,"

Miss Armstrong said, and her usually pale face looke
quite flushed.

"Well, I wouldn't advise you to go looking for th
chap, Miss Armstrong," Ann's father said, lightin
his pipe again. "It's my opinion he got a crack on th
head and is probably suffering from concussion
I dare say he'll be picked up to-morrow."

"But you have searched the area, surely," Mis
Pringle insisted.

"*I* ain't walked as far for long enough," Thomas pu
in. "We got to the point of lifting practically ever
stone . . . and there's a lot of 'em up there. If he'
wandering 'cos he got a knock on the head . . . he'
wandered pretty quick. For myself, I think he'
already well on his way out of the hills. Mebb
making for some town to lie low, and . . ."

"Thomas, Thomas," Mr. Birkett said, chuckling
"I sometimes think you'd do better leaving farming
for a job like writing detective stories." With a laugh
he turned to the two guests, adding: "I don't know
where he gets his ideas from . . . unless it's reading
the Sunday papers."

Miss Armstrong smiled, but Miss Pringle looked
very serious as she said:

"You never know, these days, Mr. Birkett. Don'
you think it odd that a man carrying so much . . . er . . .
jewellery, should vanish? Why shouldn't it have been
someone else? Someone who wasn't carrying
valuables."

"Now we're getting somewhere," Thomas chuckled.

"Let's think now. Suppose some international crook had . . ."

"It isn't a matter for joking," Miss Pringle said somewhat tartly. "As a matter of fact Miss Armstrong and I actually saw a man in the valley . . . the Brackendale valley, I mean. And we thought then that he was behaving rather oddly. He couldn't see us. We were stopped on top . . . on Tingle Crags. As a matter of fact we were watching Ann and her friend coming up the valley with the dogs. Then we saw this man."

"Well, now, it could easily have been one of the men from the village," Mr. Birkett suggested. "If he was coming up to lend a hand with the rescue . . ."

"Oh, no, no, it wasn't one of the villagers, we're sure of that," Miss Pringle interrupted eagerly. "We wouldn't have taken any notice of him. At that time we had no idea that anyone was missing from the plane, so we weren't looking for anything suspicious. What made us look twice was this man's behaviour. He was creeping round a patch of bracken. And then, almost as if he had had an idea he was being watched, he went into the bracken, and we saw no more of him."

"Perhaps Ann saw something of him," Miss Armstrong suggested. "She and Avril came up the valley."

"Did you see him?" Miss Pringle asked.

CHAPTER III

TO KEEP A PROMISE

AT ANY other time Ann would have given a "Yes" or a "No" immediately, but now her thoughts went back to their last few minutes with the stranger, Bill. Almost the final thing he had said to them before turning back up the valley had been: "If you don't mention me to anyone, that will help enormously. Can I bank on you?"

She and Avril had promised without hesitation, even though they had both thought the request a little odd. Looking up at Miss Pringle Ann wondered what excuse she could give. She did not want to tell a lie, and she could feel Miss Pringle's eyes boring into her. She opened her mouth. She must say something. And at that moment:

Crash! The silence was broken as a cup dropped to the floor and smashed into fragments. Avril had been returning her coffee cup to the table and had released it when it was only half on the table's edge.

With a gasp of dismay the French girl leapt to her feet, then knelt just as quickly to begin gathering the broken pieces, at the same time starting to offer her apologies.

42

Ann's father gave a little laugh and said to Avril: "Now, don't go worrying about that, lass. If I had all the cups I've broken they'd fill this room! There's worse things happen at sea . . . so they say, and a broken cup is better than a broken heart."

Blessing Avril for either a timely accident, or a cleverly managed interruption, Ann hurried for a cloth to mop up the coffee grains. She and Avril gathered the broken fragments with the aid of a small brush and carried them out to the dustbin.

For a moment, while one held the dustbin lid and the broken fragments were poised over the bin, the two girls looked at each other. Then Avril smiled, raised her dark eyebrows and asked:

"I am sorry for the cup, Ann; but perhaps I did right, eh?"

"I could hug you," Ann said. "I just didn't know what to say. Oh, I wouldn't like to have Miss Pringle as my form mistress. When Miss Armstrong asked me if I'd seen the man they saw, I could feel Miss Pringle's eyes boring holes into me."

Clang! The broken cup went into the dustbin and the lid was banged into place. Thomas had come out into the yard and was refilling his pipe. The sun was dropping down towards the Tingle Crag tops, and soon the Brackendale valley would be in the shadows. Somewhere a curlew was calling, its wild, rather melancholy note adding to the mysterious stillness which cloaked the mountains at the end of the day. Only the stream kept busily on, gurgling and singing over the little ford where the cattle crossed to the Long Meadow.

"What are we going to do?" Avril asked, when they were back in the kitchen, busy with the washing-up. Ann's father was out with Thomas, looking at the dipping tank through which the sheep would have to walk the next day. The two guests, Miss Pringle and Miss Armstrong were sauntering down the road in the direction of the mile-distant village.

"You keep busy with the dishes," Ann suggested, "and I'll have a look at the list of things this chap Bill wants. If we can supply them from our larder, then it won't be very difficult. To-morrow morning, when we've finished the housework, we can just have a stroll up the valley, put the things where we said we would, and that will be that."

"You do not think we should ask this Bill if he is the man from the plane?" Avril asked, a quizzical smile on her face. Then, before Ann could reply, she went on quickly: "But no. It is better that we do not know if he is the diamond thief. What we do not know we cannot tell, eh?"

"Ye—es," Ann was unfolding the slip of paper, and she frowned at the very first item on Bill's list, for it read:

"Ten pounds weight of poor quality beef."

At her little gasp of surprise, and deepening frown, Avril lifted dripping hands from the polythene wash-bowl and moved to where she, too, could look at the paper.

"Ten pounds of beef!" she exclaimed. "But . . . Ann
. . . that is a lot of beef! It is almost half a kilo in
weight. What will he do with such a lump? What
else does he want? Er . . . bread . . . butter . . . coffee . . .
sugar . . . tin milk! What is tin milk?"

"He means condensed milk," Ann explained. "Er . . .
like this," and she brought down a small tin of cream.
"It is sealed in a tin . . . like meat in a tin. It . . ."

"Ah, yes, yes," Avril exclaimed. "So he will live out
on the fell for a few days eh? But so much beef! He
must be very hungry."

Ann gently scratched her chin with a forefinger.

"I'm wondering what Mr. Chugg, the butcher, will
say when I ask him for so much in one piece. People
who keep trail-hounds buy plenty of beef, of course,
but we don't have hounds . . . only the dogs for the
sheep."

By the time they had finished washing the crockery
they had decided on a plan. After breakfast next day
Avril would take Ann's cycle and ride into Keswick.
There she would be able to buy the ten pounds of beef
without exciting suspicion. What was more she could
be sure of getting bread. Up here, at the foot of the
mountains those who did not bake their own bread
ordered it, and the baker seldom had any loaves to spare.

"And I will buy a morning newspaper, too," Avril
said excitedly. "For there must surely be a picture of
the missing man. Then we shall know for sure if this
diamond thief is our Mr. Bill. We can get newspapers
in Keswick, Ann? I . . ." And there she stopped abruptly,

for with the merest creak of a loose floorboard to warn them that someone was crossing the dining-room, Miss Pringle appeared. She tapped on the open door before halting on the threshold of the kitchen.

"Er, sorry," she said, smiling apologetically. "I hope I'm not disturbing you. I was just coming to tell you, Ann, that Miss Armstrong and I have decided to have another full day out to-morrow . . . if the weather holds good, of course."

"Oh, I'm sure it will," Ann said. "You'll want packed lunches and coffee again?"

"If you don't mind."

"I'll have everything ready immediately after breakfast," Ann promised.

Miss Pringle half-turned as if to walk back to the dining-room, then changed her mind, and turning said:

"Er . . . I couldn't help overhearing a mention of Keswick, Ann. If you are going in, I wonder if you would mind getting us the morning papers. They are one of those little luxuries we rather miss out here."

Ann and Avril exchanged quick glances. Then Ann nodded.

"Of course. Avril is just dying to have a look at Keswick by daylight . . . and as I shall be busy for most of the morning I am lending her my bike. If you'll jot down what papers you want . . . she'll try to get them."

"That's very kind of you," Miss Pringle said, coming into the kitchen and looking round for a scrap of paper. "To be quite honest, Ann, we're just dying to get hold of a paper. There's sure to be a picture of the missing man in it, and you know . . . we . . . well, it's Miss Armstrong, really, she feels sure that the man we saw earlier to-day *must* be the missing man. She . . . well, as we said during dinner, we both felt that he acted rather suspiciously."

She scribbled down the list of morning papers she wanted, gave Avril enough to cover their cost, smiled and went out. After a few moments Avril gave a slow, very expressive shrug, so comical that Ann burst out laughing.

"I think," Avril said quietly, "that all school-mistresses must be trained to be detectives, Ann. Our Miss Pringle, she is like a bloodhound, sniffing round for clues. What shall we do if the newspapers show pictures of the missing man, and he *is* Bill?"

It was Ann's turn to shrug and look perplexed.

"I suppose we should really walk down to the village and tell Constable Johnson, then . . ."

"Oh, Ann!" Avril exclaimed, flouncing round the table excitedly, "how can you say such a thing? He saves us from a . . . predicament. Maybe he saves me from more than a predicament; maybe he saves me from breaking my neck. And . . . my dear Ann, it is the only neck I have. So . . ."

"Yes," Ann agreed. "Well, I don't know. I think the best thing is to wait until we see the morning papers. Come on, I'll take you down to our pool. With the light going like this I'll try and show you how to tickle for trout."

They went out. The sun had now dropped below Tingle Crags. There was a soft blueness about the top of Brackendale valley. The sheep waiting for their annual dip, were for the most part grazing quietly in the paddock, with one or two bleating soberly. It was a scene of peace.

Down the stream for quarter of a mile the two girls went, and there, where the babbling water widened out into a pool, and all was quiet, Ann tried to teach her French pen-friend how to "tickle" for trout.

When the last red of the sun was dying from the clouds overhead, Avril got from her knees and wiped her right hand dry. She shook her head ruefully as she said:

"I think there are some things which cannot be taught, Ann; and this *tickling* for fishes is one of them. *You* put in your hand . . . hold your fingers below the the surface, and then . . . flip . . . and there is a lovely little brown fish on the bank. I put *my* hand in . . . I wait . . . I flip, and all I do is splash water into my eyes. The trout have swum away to tell their friends about the silly French girl who tries to tickle them."

"Well, there are four who won't be laughing," Ann reminded her, pointing to the four, brown speckled beauties lying on the grass. "You'll enjoy these at breakfast to-morrow. Now we'd better get back to the house. Father and Thomas always like a mug of tea before going to bed."

It was an early start for everyone next day. Avril

rose with Ann, and watched the milking of the few cows kept at Brackendale. There was a freshness about the air which soon changed as the sun began to show its power. The signs were all of another hot day, with only a suggestion of breeze.

Ann's father and Thomas were soon out dipping the sheep, and when they came to the kitchen for breakfast brought with them a strong smell of disinfectant. Breakfast for the guests was already over, for Miss Pringle and Miss Armstrong had also risen early, meaning to spend a very full day on the fells.

At nine o'clock Avril went off on Ann's cycle, a small rucksack strapped on to the cycle carrier. Miss Pringle watched her go down the not very smooth track, then went back into the house to ask how long the French girl would be.

"I'd love to see the morning papers before we left," she said. "They're bound to carry pictures of the missing man . . . bound to."

"And we're more convinced than ever that the man we saw yesterday was the very man," Miss Armstrong added. "Just think, Ann; if we found him. There's sure to be a big reward offered for the missing diamonds. If we found him . . . and the diamonds of course, well . . ." and closing her eyes she shook her head as if the very thought of such a reward left her dazed.

Ann was silent for a moment as she busied herself packing the sandwiches for lunch. She had been half-hoping that their guests would not go up the Brackendale valley again; but it seemed as if that was what they had in mind.

"It might not be so pleasant if you did find him," she suggested. "Suppose he had died from exposure. People who get lost in the mountains do die that way."

"Oh, Ann, what rubbish," Miss Pringle said, laughing scornfully. "Exposure . . .! At this season of the year? And in such marvellous weather as this? Come, come, Ann, you know better than that. It almost sounds as if you don't want us to go up Brackendale to-day?"

She was smiling, but when Ann looked up from the sandwiches she was packing, she experienced a queer little shock as she looked for a moment into Miss Pringle's grey-green eyes. She felt Miss Pringle was looking right into her very mind, probing for the secret she and Avril held.

"I . . . it doesn't matter to me where you go," she said, flustered. "All I was thinking was that you would most likely be disappointed. After all . . . experienced men like Father and Thomas have searched, haven't they?"

"Yes, but not in Brackendale," Miss Pringle pointed out. "Apparently the police did not think the man would come over here. And, if he did, they reckoned he would have come right down the valley. Well . . . you and Avril were in the valley, weren't you; and you didn't see him. So . . ."

"We think he is still up there," Miss Armstrong

chipped in excitedly. "And we don't think he's ill, either. We think he's . . ."

"Of course, what we think doesn't matter, Joyce," Miss Pringle cut in, at which Miss Armstrong flinched and said no more.

Ann packed their rucksacks, and going to the door watched them walk out on to the track leading up the valley; then she returned to the house. There was much to do before she was free to rush off with Avril to deliver the things Bill had asked them to buy for him.

After washing the crockery she made the beds, dusted, cooled the morning's milk and collected the eggs. She prepared a cold meal for her father and Thomas, and then cut sandwiches for herself and Avril. She kept at it in such a fury that she was amazed when she heard a sudden tingle-lingle-lingle-ling from the yard, announcing the return of a hot-looking Avril.

"I boil. I die of exhaustion," Avril panted. "Ann, these mountain roads are bewitched. I ride into Keswick, and every part of the road seems to lead up a hill. I think . . . well, never mind, I shall ride without pedalling all the way back. But no . . . while I am in the beautiful little town of Keswick someone changes the roads. They all become uphill for the way back. I die of exhaustion. Here, Ann . . . try one of these. I bought half a pound in Keswick. If we do not eat them they will melt." And she produced a half-pound box of chocolates.

She sank into a chair, fanning herself vigorously. Ann brought a face cloth and Avril leaned back, eyes closed, while her face was cooled and dried. Then she opened the box of chocolates.

"You are an angel, Ann. Try one. They are very good. Each time I have to stop on a hill I take a chocolate to build up my strength again. And when you feel the weight of that box on the cycle . . . then you will know that I need my strength building again."

Ann helped herself to a chocolate, then unstrapped the big cardboard carton which had been tied to the cycle carrier. She blinked at its weight as she carried it into the kitchen. When she opened the carton the reason for its weight was apparent at once. Surrounded by bread, butter, sugar and coffee was a great lump of beef. She whistled softly as she lifted it out. Ten pounds! It felt more like twenty. Then she began taking the other things out, stopping at sight of a packet of twenty cigarettes. She turned to look at Avril, her eyebrows raised in a silent question.

Her friend shook her head, laughing.

"No, no, Ann. *I* do not smoke. I think of this Bill of ours, and I say to myself. He is a man; he smokes cigarettes; he will have none left, so . . . these."

" And what about the papers? Did you . . ." Ann stopped at the sound of swift footsteps in the house. In a matter of moments Miss Pringle and Miss Armstrong were standing together in the kitchen doorway.

" Did you get the morning papers?" Miss Pringle

asked, her eyes on the rolled-up bundle of papers Avril had been in the act of taking out of the big carton.

"I thought you would have been over Tingle Crags by this time," Ann said, taken aback at sight of their visitors. "Aren't you going, after all?"

"Well, yes," Miss Pringle said apologetically. "We did intend making a real day of it, but stopped for a little while to watch the sheep-dipping, and then Miss Armstrong suggested that as Avril could not possibly be away much longer, we might as well stay to see the papers. We're really very interested in this missing man."

"And after all," Miss Armstrong said, "if we met him and we hadn't seen his photograph, we wouldn't know him, would we? We'd look rather silly if we stopped a stranger on the fells and asked him if he was the missing man. He might be a searcher, mightn't he?" and she laughed a little self-consciously.

Avril handed over the bundle of papers, and it was not until Miss Pringle and Miss Armstrong had really left the farmhouse that Ann remembered their own morning paper.

"Oh, thump, Avril. Was our paper in the bundle?"

Avril gasped, her shoulders slumped, and then as quickly she brightened up again.

"It does not matter, Ann, it just does not matter. I looked through every paper . . . but there is not a picture of the missing man. Well, there is one of him taken many years ago . . . when he was just growing up. No picture of him as he is to-day."

"Oh! So we still don't know whether Bill is the man or not," Ann said ruefully.

"But we know something else," Avril said, her eyes gleaming with excitement. "The diamonds this man carries are worth . . . guess how much; just guess how much?"

"How can I?" Ann said, looking critically at the huge lump of beef. Bill had said "poor quality" beef and Avril had certainly got that.

"Two hundred thousand pounds," Avril almost whispered the words. "I have been working it out in French francs. It is two and a half million new francs, at least. And there is a reward!"

"Well, don't gloat like that," Ann said, beginning to laugh. "You look as if we are going to march up the fell, grab Bill, and run him down to the police station in a matter of minutes."

"Non, non!" Avril protested. "I do not wish to do that at all," and bringing out a wisp of a handkerchief began again to mop her hot face. "I am worried, Ann, very worried. You know . . . I think Bill *is* the missing man. I am sure he is. Do you not think so?"

It was Ann's turn to look serious. She, too, sat down. On the table before them was the big, solid hunk of beef; the bread, butter, coffee, sugar, tinned milk and cigarettes. All the items bought for the man who had helped them out of a tight corner; and who had then asked them to help him. Both girls had a feeling that he must be the man for whom everyone had been searching.

"We must decide what to do," Avril said quietly. "Shall we go to the people in authority, the police; or shall we . . .?"

She stopped, for Ann was shaking her head, slowly but with emphasis.

"We can't give him away like that," she said. "Avril, he helped us, and we gave him our word that we would keep quiet; we said we would take him this beef and the other things. I know we can't stop Miss Pringle and her friend from telling the police if they spot him . . ."

Avril leant over the table.

"I think if you had agreed that we divide on him . . ." Avril began, then stopped, puzzled. "No, that is not it. There is a word for this informing on someone. It is divide, maybe cut up."

She frowned, then suddenly smiled and chuckled as Ann supplied the missing word:

"You mean if we *split* on . . ."

"Ah, so, so; that is it," Avril agreed. "I think if you had agreed to split on this M'sieur Bill, then I shall not feel very friendly with you any more. But how can I imagine you would do the wrong thing, eh? We think alike eh? We are twins. *You* agree. *I* agree. So, we take this mountain of beef and the other things to our so all-alone Bill, and we shall tell him the police search for him. We shall say there is a reward, and, oh!" and she gasped, "I forget to tell you. There is a reward for the person who finds this satchel with the diamonds. Five thousand pounds!"

"Five thousand pounds. Golly! That's going to make Miss Armstrong keener than ever," Ann said, pulling a face. "I wish they weren't staying here, Avril. If they discovered Bill they'd feel they ought to report to the police at once. And the trouble is they're right on the spot where they might easily find him."

"Aah, they will never find him," Avril insisted, "I have the feeling in my bones that he will get away. Come . . . can we go now? Or must we wait until our two lady detectives have gone over the fell?"

"We're going to have some coffee," Ann said. "And what's more, if I don't take Father and Thomas a big jug of tea, and their ' elevenses ' they'll be in here wanting to know what has gone wrong."

She made a jug of coffee and a much bigger jug of tea. Leaving Avril to continue cooling off, Ann took the tea and half a dozen buttered scones out to the dipping paddock. There was a bedlam of noise from the sheep who had yet to be dipped, and splashes from those being hustled into the stone trough.

Thomas, wearing rubber thigh-boots, was standing in the "dip", and making sure that every Herdwick which Mr. Birkett heaved into the tank was well and truly soused with the disinfectant. It was hard, hot and tiring work, and both men were glad of an excuse to rest for a few minutes.

Ann poured two mugs of tea and, while she waited, suggested to her father that she and Avril would take those sheep which had been dipped, on to the fells and so get them out of the way.

"Now? What about lunch?"

"It's all laid out," Ann assured him. "All you have to do is pop the kettle on and warm the tea-pot."

"You see, boss," Thomas said, a twinkle in his eyes, "she comes here to offer to take the sheep, but she's already decided she's going to do it. Got something in mind, she has, you can be sure. Bet they're going up to the crashed plane to look for souvenirs."

"How wrong you are, Thomas," Ann said, poking out her tongue at him. They were very good friends and the old man loved to tease her. "We've no intention of going anywhere near the crash. Of course, if you'd rather take the sheep up when you've finished dipping, I don't mind. Avril and I can sit in the shade and rest."

"That makes me more certain than ever that they're just looking for an excuse to get away from the farm," Thomas said, blowing lustily on his tea to cool it a little and winking at Mr. Birkett. "There's something hatching, boss, mark my words. What's the little French girl been down to Keswick for? She looked like a boiled lobster when she got back."

"If I told you what she went for you wouldn't believe me," Ann said pertly, "so I won't tell you. Daddy, do you want the sheep out now, or will they all go together later?"

"Yes, take those that have been dipped," her father said, "and start them up the Long Face fell. We don't want too many of them in the valley for a day or two. There's the Hound Trail on to-morrow, y'know."

While they had been talking Avril had joined them, and she turned eagerly to say:

"Hound Trail! Ah, I shall love that. I have seen pictures of the hounds and the men on horses, men wearing bright red coats. They will hunt for foxes to-morrow, yes?"

"Foxes!" Thomas looked up and chuckled as he shook his head. "There's no hunting of anything at a Hound Trail, Miss Avril. A Hound Trail is a sort of race, a test of wind and legs and noses."

"Ah, you pull my leg," Avril chuckled. "Whoever heard of a test of noses? What is this test, eh? You try to make a fool of me, I am sure."

Thomas shook his head and finishing his mug of tea in one noisy gulp put his pint pot on the grass then began feeling for his pipe. Very solemnly he assured her:

"When you've seen a Hound Trail, Miss Avril, you'll have seen something you can't see nowhere else in the wide world; but there won't be anybody wearing red coats. And if there are any horses about, they'll have come because they've been harnessed to a dog-cart, or something like that."

Avril turned to Ann, a look of bewilderment on her face.

"But, Ann, I have read about this business of hounds. There was a famous man who had a hunting horn.

John Peel I think, he was called. There was a song . . .
but I cannot remember it now."

"Oh, aye," Thomas agreed. "Was this the song?:
   ' D'ye ken John Peel wi' his coat so gay?
    D'ye ken John Peel at the break o' the day?'
Is that the song?"

Avril nodded eagerly.

"Yes, that is it. There was something in it about
' At the break of the day, with his hounds and his
horse in the morning.' Was he not a Hound
Trailer?"

"Not hounds and horse, Avril. Hounds and horn!"
Ann's father said, chuckling. "There are packs of
hounds which hunt the foxes; but a Hound Trail is
different. It is a kind of race. Thomas said it was
a test of wind and legs and noses. He was quite right.
You see a trail is laid by means of a bag filled with
aniseed. Two men will drag it over the ground
to-morrow. They'll start from our Long Meadow,
go up the valley, round the top, and back again . . .
and they'll leave the scent of aniseed on the grass and
the ground. That's where the test of noses comes in.
You see, when the signal is given all the hounds start
off, nose to the ground. They have to follow the
scent of the aniseed. The first hound to go round
the course and get back to the starting point is the
winner. The hounds are wonderfully fit. They have
to be. Strong in the legs and strong in the lungs.
You'll enjoy it, I think. It's quite exciting, I can tell
you."

" There is no fox to catch?" asked Avril amazed.

"No, it's just a race," Ann's father said, smiling. "You'll understand better when you see it. There won't be any quietness in this valley on Thursday, I can tell you, and no loneliness, either. The hounds are brought from all over the Lake district."

"Aye, you'll have a rare tale to tell when you gets back to Paris," Thomas assured her, and picking up his empty mug he handed it to Ann, then walked away towards the dipping trough.

"Don't go tiring Avril," Ann's father said, as he put his mug on the tray. "You know she may not be as accustomed to fell walking as you."

"Daddy," Ann protested, "you know I told you Avril climbs real mountains. Anyway we shan't rush. We're taking some lunch with us, but we'll be home for tea-time, so you needn't worry. Everything is ready for when I get back, and our guests won't be coming back until evening."

Back in the farmhouse they packed the food and the beef into two rucksacks, hoping that even the sharp-eyed Thomas would have no excuse for asking awkward questions if he saw them. Even so the rucksacks bulged. With a ten pound chunk of beef in one, plus a tin of coffee and a tin of condensed milk, while the other rucksack held loaves, et cetera, plus a small kettle, a cup, plate and spoon, there was no hiding the fact that they were carrying much more than sandwiches and a flask.

Thomas and Mr. Birkett were very busy, however,

and hardly looked up when Ann called Shep and Nell to round up the dipped sheep while she opened the gate which gave on to the fell track.

Filling the air with their bleating, more than a hundred ewes jostled their way through the gate and headed for the freedom of the fells. They were all eager to get back on the heights, and there was little work for the two dogs until the Milestone Pen was reached. This was a rough stone shelter in which sheep could gather for protection against the withering wintry blasts. It was from this spot, where several small streams came bustling down over rocks and through patches of bracken, that the real climbing began.

It was one o'clock before the Herdwicks were safely up the Long Face fell, scattered and now grazing on the thin grass. The dogs came back to Ann and Avril who had reached the place where they had agreed to leave Bill's supplies. It was at a spot where a huge area of bracken began.

With rucksacks open they laid out the bread, butter, coffee, et cetera, and the big lump of beef. Avril opened their sandwiches as the two dogs, tongues lolling, sat hopefully watching her.

"Not one scrap, Avril," Ann ordered. "They know it isn't any use looking at me; but they're cute, you know. They can tell by the expression on your face that you would like to feed them; but they are not to have a single crumb. They're the best beggars in the Lake Countries, and . . ."

"We are being watched," Avril interrupted, gaily tossing a piece of meat sandwich to each dog.

"Watched?" Ann queried. "By whom?"

"Look up towards the high rocks at the head of here . . ."

"Tingle Crags. They . . . oh, yes. I can see it. You mean the sun shining on glasses. Hm!" Ann laid a restraining hand on Avril's arm as she was about to toss another sandwich to the expectant dogs. "No more, Avril, please. It spoils them. Do you know who I think it will be?"

"Give me three guesses," Avril chuckled. "Maybe I am right first guess, eh? I think it is our Miss Armstrong and Miss Pringle."

"They've gone to the one spot where they can watch the whole valley," Ann said thoughtfully. "You know I . . . Nell, heel, heel. What's the matter with you?"

Nell and Shep had suddenly ceased to be interested in Avril's sandwiches, and were now on their feet and staring intently at the bracken. Its fringe was a matter of a few yards' distance, and the belt ran right up the valley, almost to the foot of Tingle Crags.

"They are frightened," Avril whispered, astonished. "What is it? See . . . the hair on the back it stands up. That is always a sign of fear. What can frighten them, Ann?"

Ann pushed her rucksack from across her out-stretched legs and got to her knees. Now the two dogs were slowly backing towards her. They had every sign of retreating from some danger. They were growling softly. The hair on the back of their shoulders was ruffed up; the bushy tails, usually carried so high were down; down between their legs. A sure sign that they were frightened.

"What's the matter, Nell?" Ann laid a hand gently on the sheep-dog's back and at her touch Nell quivered, a sure sign of nervousness. Yet there was nothing to be seen. A gentle breeze was blowing down the fell, and stirring the bracken fronds. It brought to the girls the warm, earthy smell which the sun draws out of bracken. There was, however, another scent which went unnoticed by Ann and her friend, but it was pungent enough to Nell and Shep. It was that scent which was scaring them.

The dogs continued to stand and stare at the bracken fringe. Looking in the same direction both Ann and Avril noticed the same thing at exactly the same moment. One patch of bracken a few yards from the edge of the patch was moving more than the rest. It was as if something was forcing its way through the mass of foliage, dividing it as a plough divides earth.

Then Shep took a pace forward. He was stiff-legged now, his hackles were up and his tail had lifted a little. Had Ann been able to look into her dog's eyes she would have seen they were green as emeralds: sign of both fear and anger. He gave a low, challenging growl.

Ann had only heard him growl like that in the past when there had been a strange dog near the house, and usually when the strange dog was a big one. Shep growled again, and then Nell went forward as if to support him. Her tail was down, but she was obeying the training which had started when she was a puppy—to defend against any danger, anything in her charge. At this moment it was not a flock of sheep she was defending, but her mistress.

"Shep . . . Nell, come back," Ann's voice was sharp with fear now. The waving fronds of bracken hid something out of the ordinary, and that unknown creature was now within a yard or so of the open.

Both sheep-dogs halted. Nell cast a quick glance over her shoulder in the direction of Ann. She whined, as if apologising for not obeying the order. Then moved on another foot to be shoulder to shoulder with Shep.

At that moment there came a ringing shout from up the fellside.

"Call your dogs back. Do you hear, call them back. Don't let them go into the bracken. *Don't let them go into the bracken!*"

Even as the words began to echo and re-echo across the valley, there came from the bracken itself a short, coughing bark. It was not the bark of a dog. It was almost a roar, and the menace in it halted even the brave Shep. His tail drooped a little. Nell leapt back a yard, and for a moment seemed about to race off down the fell. After a moment, she steadied, looked up at Ann as if asking for orders, then fell in line with Shep once more. As she did so the silence was broken again by that frightening half-cough, half-roar.

The fronds of bracken only a yard or so from the edge of the patch swayed in agitated fashion and Avril, grabbing Ann by the arm, whispered tensely:

"It . . . it's coming out."

CHAPTER IV

BILL PLEADS FOR A FRIEND

Above them there was a clatter, and a man who had started down the long scree left a grey scar on the stony slope as he took a wilder leap than before to keep his balance, and started a small avalanche of stones clattering down with him.

Both girls heard the sound, but neither dared take her eyes off the bracken for fear the unseen creature might come out. They could just make out a form, but it was only vague, almost shadowy.

Ann, who had seen fell foxes many a time, knew this was no fox. By the amount of bracken which moved, the thing must be several times as long as any hill fox, and was certainly far bolder.

There was a sudden cessation of clattering from the scree above, and Avril chancing a quick look upwards, groaned, and whispered:

"He has fallen!"

Ann did not look up. The movements of the creature in the fringe of the bracken was mesmerising her. In a way she was reminded of a visit she had once made to the zoo. Fascinated, she had stood before the cage of a mighty Bengal tiger. Supple, silent, sinuous in its movements, the tiger had paced across the front of its cage first to one end then to the other. When it reached one end it wheeled in a swift, graceful about-turn, and walked back the way it had come. It was a jungle hunter in captivity, padding backwards and forwards, backwards and forwards. This creature in the bracken was doing exactly the same thing; but it was not in a cage.

"I . . . I . . . Avril," Ann whispered, and her voice was little more than a croak, "I . . . think it is a tiger!"

It was a fantastic thing to suggest, but even as a startled Avril turned to see if Ann was joking, there came another shout from the man above them. High up on the scree though he was, they recognised his voice, now. He was shouting, slowly and deliberately, and it was the man they had met the day before. The man who called himself Bill. In a slow bellow he yelled:

"Throw . . . him . . . the . . . meat! Throw . . . him . . . the . . . meat!"

In the slumbrous quiet of that sun-drenched valley, with rocky hills on three sides, the words were picked up and flung from one side to the other in a series of echoes and re-echoes. After the first clear-cut command of "Throw him the meat" the echoes became blurred, words piling on words, with only the last two sounding clearly. Time after time they sounded, each time a little fainter:

" . . . the . . . meat . . . the . . . meat . . . the . . . m—e—a—t."

The hills tossed the words about until finally only a faraway whisper could be heard . . . "meat!"

High up on Tingle Crags Miss Pringle and Miss Armstrong had been sitting in the lee of a big rock, sheltering from the breeze, and able to enjoy to the full the sunshine and an uninterrupted view of the Brackendale valley. They had with them Miss Armstrong's field-glasses, and after they had eaten their packed lunch they had scanned the valley in turn through the powerful lenses.

They had watched Ann Birkett and Avril Leresche come up the valley with the two dogs and the flock of new-dipped sheep. It was a very ordinary scene enlivened for the watchers only when Miss Pringle said:

"Hm! Joyce, look at the rucksacks they carry. Why two? Surely they can only be carrying a few sandwiches. You'd think they were starting a week's hike, or something. By the way the French girl walks I would say her rucksack contained something pretty heavy."

She held out the glasses, and before focusing them Miss Armstrong murmured:

"The word *heavy* reminds me. What did you make of that horrible great lump of beef on the kitchen table this morning. I hope they're not going to offer me any of it. It looked simply awful stuff. Up here one rather expects to get fresh lamb. That piece looked ghastly."

She put the field-glasses to her eyes, and for a few moments there was nothing out of the ordinary to see. The sheep had gone to the Long Face fell. The two dogs had come back and were obviously begging from Avril. Then, for no apparent reason, the scene changed.

The dogs whipped round to face the bracken. Within seconds Ann and Avril were on their feet, and sensing something out of the ordinary Miss Pringle insisted on taking the field-glasses.

Both women were now on their feet, and Miss Pringle looked like some general watching a vital battle, completely ignoring her friend's pleas for a comment on what was happening. Finally, and she spoke in a breathless whisper, she said:

"Joyce . . . I'm sure something dreadful is going to happen. There's something in the bracken down there. I can see a gap . . . and it's moving. There's something creeping through the bracken towards those two girls."

"It'll be the man from the plane," Miss Armstrong gasped. "Do you think we . . . I wonder . . . ought we to . . . Jean, please, what is happening? Tell me or lend me the glasses. They *are* mine!"

She even reached out as if to take the field-glasses, but Miss Pringle was so tense that she simply pushed her friend away, and continued to stare down at the patch of bracken some five hundred feet or so below their eyrie.

Finally she whispered:

"There *is* somebody crawling through the bracken, Joyce. I was only guessing at first, but near the fringe the bracken is not so dense, and I saw something moving. I'm absolutely certain it will be the man from the plane. Those girls knew all about him. Why should they come to exactly that spot, eh? He . . . all right, all right, take the glasses," she said angrily, and thrust them into her friend's hands. "Nothing is going to happen. They've stopped by the bracken so that he can come out without being too conspicuous. Well, *we* can see them, and . . ."

"Jean . . . there's a man coming down the scree. To the right . . . above them. If he . . . oh, he's fallen!"

Miss Armstrong only blinked when her friend snatched the glasses from her, and for perhaps ten seconds neither woman spoke. Then Miss Pringle broke the silence with a puzzled:

"Well, if the missing man is in the bracken . . . who is the man on the scree?" She directed the glasses towards the bracken again; noted the patch where something was moving; it was now close to the edge, only a matter of yards from the two girls and their dogs. Then she looked over to the scree again. The man who had been lunging down, only to fall, was on his feet again, and so powerful were the glasses that Miss Pringle gave a little gasp as she recognised Bill. "Joyce . . . the man on the scree is the one we saw yesterday. I'm almost sure it's him, and . . ."

"Throw . . . him . . . the . . . meat. Throw . . . him . . . the . . . meat!"

The command came hollowly across the air, and in a matter of seconds was being blurred by echoes.

"Throw him . . . what?" Miss Pringle asked sharply. Miss Armstrong had gone quite pale, and she moistened her dry lips before saying:

"I . . . I . . . thought he said ' meat '!"

"Throw him the meat!" Miss Pringle said, shocked. "Joyce . . . JOYCE . . . it isn't a man in the bracken. You wouldn't throw meat to a man, would you?" Like her friend, she too went pale at the thought of what might be down there, hidden by the waving green fronds.

Backwards and forwards across the valley went the echoing words . . . "the . . . meat . . . the meat . . . the . . . meat . . . m—e—a—t!"

"She's thrown something!" Miss Armstrong had taken the glasses from the trembling hands of her friend, and had focused them. "Ann picked something off the ground and threw . . . oh!"

"What? What's the matter now?" Miss Pringle was shaking.

"It's just occurred to me. The meat . . . the great lump of meat we saw on the table. That will be what Ann threw. She . . . oh, the man on the scree is going down to them."

Miss Armstrong focused the glasses carefully on the scree while her friend watched and waited. She was almost holding her breath until in a sudden flurry of words Miss Armstrong broke the silence with:

"Yes, I'm sure now that it is the same man! You

were right. He's reached them, and . . . oh, he's leaving them. He's running into the bracken, and . . ." Then there was a pause.

"Well? Well? What's happening?" Miss Pringle could hardly restrain herself.

Lowering the glasses for a moment Miss Armstrong stood and stared at her friend, then in a shocked whisper said:

"He's gone . . . vanished."

Down below, Ann and Avril were almost as shocked. Ann, obeying the command from Bill, now hurrying down the scree, bent and grabbed the lump of beef. With all the strength she could muster she raised it high and threw it, as a footballer might take a "throw-in", tossing the meat towards the bracken, over the heads of the two sheep-dogs.

It was a good throw, and the big piece of meat hit the sun-baked ground only a foot or so from the edge of the bracken. It bounced a little soggily, and rolled into the first of the gently waving fronds.

There was a sudden snarl; the bracken waved violently; a powerful looking paw, tawny in colour, shot out and the meat was scooped out of sight. Just for a moment the two girls caught a glimpse of a triangular shaped head, and two eyes as green as the eyes of Shep and Nell. The bracken waved even more violently and then the turmoil ceased.

"It's gone," Ann said, and with her legs suddenly weak as watered milk, she dropped to her knees.

The two dogs charged right to the edge of the bracken, but halted there, and after a moment, retreated, without turning their backs on the yard-high foliage as if they feared the unknown might return and leap on them.

Avril remained standing. Not because she felt any better than Ann, but because she was afraid to move. The trembling which had begun inside her had now communicated itself to her knees and her arms. She clasped her hands tightly, but her knees just shook.

Then with a clatter of small stones rolling down with him, Bill arrived. One knee of his trousers was torn, as a result of his fall on the scree. His right hand was bleeding where the skin had been badly grazed in the same fall, and he was panting wildly.

"Are you all right?" he demanded, and when a swift glance at both girls assured him they appeared to be none the worse for their experience of the past minute or so he asked: "Where did he go? Where was he?"

Ann pointed, not daring to trust her voice.

"All right, I'll get after him. Stay here. I won't be long." Even as he was speaking Bill was dragging from his coat pocket a long, shining chain. There was a stout leather collar on one end, a looped handle on the other.

Without another word he plunged into the bracken, and the luxuriant growth came just above his waist. At this spot, with one or two small rills pouring down off the fells, the bracken always grew thicker and higher than in most other places.

Ann scrambled to her feet, and now her heart was pounding again. She wanted to shout, and warn him against the animal which had scooped up the ten-pound lump of beef with such ease, but for a moment no words would come. Avril moved to her side and gripped Ann's right hand.

"It is foolish," she gasped. "The danger . . ." and there she stopped, for the figure plunging through the bracken had vanished. One moment he was there and the next he was gone. Nor was there any shout of fear or dismay.

Both girls were panting, hearts thumping wildly. They were remembering that powerful paw, the tawny head with the green shining eyes. Then, and it made them close their eyes with relief, they heard Bill call:

"Hallo . . .! Hi . . .! Give me a hand."

Shep growled. Nell rubbed herself against Ann's right leg, as if trying to warn her not to attempt anything foolish. Ann started to run, and Avril was only a pace behind her. The two dogs followed, their lips wrinkling back in silent snarls as they reached the edge of the bracken and got the scent of the animal which their instinct had warned them was far too big and dangerous for them to tackle.

"Shout again," Ann yelled, and was answered within seconds.

"Watch out, now; watch out," Bill yelled. "There's a stream runs through here and I walked straight into it."

They found him sitting in the bed of the stream

below the level of the ground. The bracken cut off the brilliant sunlight, so that bending down to him gave the impression of being in a miniature jungle.

The stream bed was only about two feet deep; a fissure cut in the hillside by a swift running rill. Nor was it more than a yard wide; but Bill had apparently stepped right into the middle of it. Plunging one foot on to a stone which turned he had ricked an ankle rather badly. The pain of it had drained the colour from his face.

He sat there, fretting and fuming as he gently moved his foot this way and that to make sure no bones were broken. The pain was sharp, and finally he allowed the two girls to help him to his feet and out into the open. The bracken was no place for anyone to sit, for it was teeming with minute flies and insects of all kinds. In addition it exuded a steamy heat which had them all perspiring freely by the time they got back to where they had left the two rucksacks. Almost as if they had agreed not to ask any awkward questions for the time being, Ann and Avril remained as silent as Bill.

When they got him seated Avril dived a hand into the outer pocket of her rucksack and produced the packet of cigarettes she had purchased that morning.

"Here," she said triumphantly. "Always, in the stories I read, wounded men are given a cigarette while they wait for the doctor. You will smoke, yes?"

Bill was wiping perspiration from his forehead, but he paused and a smile chased the grim look away.

"Thank *you*," he said with emphasis. "I may not be wounded, but this is one of those times when I really need a smoke. I ran out of cigarettes just after sunrise. Have you got a match?"

Avril gave him a light while Ann poured coffee from the vacuum flask they had brought along.

"I say this is first rate," Bill said. "It seems years since I had a hot drink. Hm! Very nice. Who made the coffee? It's just like Continental coffee. Did you make it?" and he looked at Avril, who promptly shook her head.

Ann brought water in the sou'wester she always carried in her rucksack, and insisted on bathing Bill's badly scratched hand. She bandaged it, though he protested that it was only a scratch.

"Have you been inoculated against tetanus recently?" Ann asked.

Bill paused in the act of taking another drink and looked at her startled.

"Inoculated against tetanus?" he asked. "No. Why?"

"Then don't fuss about having your scratch bandaged," Ann said. "Wherever animals graze there is a risk of tetanus if you get a scratch and get dirt in it from the ground. I'm going to put some disinfectant on the bandage . . . and when it soaks through the lint it will smart."

"Pour away," Bill ordered, "and thanks again."

He blinked when the disinfectant seeped through to his lacerated palm, but that was the only sign he gave that the wound was "smarting".

A wet bandage was put about his ankle, and then Ann took the cup of coffee Avril had poured for her. The French girl had unwrapped the sandwiches they had brought, and handed them round. After that there was an awkward silence finally broken by Bill.

"You've got the real hospital technique, haven't you," he chuckled. "All the ward discipline, sit up and shut up, eh? Anyway, I'm mighty glad you were here. Though I suppose I wouldn't have come rushing down like I did if you hadn't come, would I? Trouble was— if the dogs had gone into the bracken . . ." and he shrugged.

"What was it?" Ann put the question both she and Avril had been dying to ask, and a tiny shiver ran through her as she remembered again that powerful paw, with the claws shining dully in the sun, and the green, lambent glow in the animal's eyes. "It almost looked like a lion. Though of course I know there are no lions within miles of . . ."

"But there are," Bill interrupted, and both girls stared at him, not quite sure whether to laugh in scorn at his words, or believe him.

"You make a joke?" Avril suggested.

"No," Bill shook his head slowly, popped the last of his sandwich into his mouth and chewed for a few moments as if pondering. Then, making up his mind, he looked them squarely in the face and said: "You can laugh at this if you like, but it happens to be true. I am a *lion-tamer!*"

"*What?*"

"And Felix . . . the animal that took the beef . . . is my best lion. Actually he isn't a lion in the ordinary sense of the word. He doesn't come from Africa. He's a mountain lion from America, and his proper name is cougar."

The news left the two girls shocked into complete silence. The very thought that they had been a matter of yards distant from a lion—or cougar—left them both with a cold feeling in the stomach.

As if he realised their thoughts, Bill went on smoothly:

"Mind you, don't get the idea that he's dangerous. He isn't one of your wild man-eating lions, or anything like that. Felix was born in captivity, and up to four days ago had never known what it was to be free. We'd arrived at a spot where the circus was to stay for a few days, and were busy putting up the big top when some idiot opened the door of Felix's cage. Or at least removed the lock. I was going the rounds just before turning in, and as I got near the cage Felix did what he usually does, reared up against the door . . . and that was that."

"The door opened?" Avril whispered.

"With a rush, and Felix *fell* out. He just gave one flabbergasted snarl, and was off. I was so shaken that it was half a minute before I realised I'd lost my best performing cat."

"Cat? M'sieur . . . you say cat?" Avril asked. "But a moment ago you say this Felix is a lion."

"Er . . . oh, yes," Bill grinned a little awkwardly.

"In the circus we call them the big cats. Anyway, Felix is a mountain lion . . . which is the reason why I am here in these hills, and why I asked you yesterday not to tell anyone I was here."

Ann frowned.

"I'm afraid I don't understand," she confessed.

"Hm! You will," Bill said grimly. "What do you think would happen if word got out that a circus lion had escaped and was in these mountains? Just think for a moment."

"I know!" Avril said eagerly. "The people would not come into the mountains. The holiday people! That is it, eh?"

"Not really," Bill shook his head. "Once the police got to know, they'd get as many men with guns as they could . . . and there'd be a hunt. They wouldn't believe any story about Felix being harmless. The next thing would be a dead mountain lion . . . and me out of a job. Felix is the best performer I have ever had, and without him my circus act is done for."

There was a short silence, with Ann and Avril exchanging glances, then Ann said:

"Do you know why we thought you wanted us to keep quiet? We thought you were from the crashed plane."

It was Bill's turn to look surprised.

"But that doesn't make sense. If I was from the crashed plane, why should I want to hang about the fells, without food or a tent? After all . . ."

"There is a very good reason," Ann interposed.

"You see, a man is missing from the plane, and he's taken with him a satchel of diamonds . . . a hundred . . . how much was it, Avril?"

"I think the newspaper said the diamonds were valued at two hundred thousand pounds!"

"What!" Bill gaped at the two girls, looking first at one and then the other as if to try and catch a grin; but they were both serious-eyed. "You mean to tell me that somebody from the crashed plane has walked off with two hundred thousand quid's worth of diamonds? Oh, come off it. Whose leg are you pulling?"

"Whose leg are *you* pulling when you tell us you are a lion-tamer, and that the animal we saw was a mountain lion?" Ann asked pertly.

"I'm telling you the gospel truth," Bill said stoutly.

"We speak the truth, too," Avril snapped. "And I tell you this, M'sieur Bill . . ."

"Listen . . . cut out the ' M'sieur'. I'm Bill Leaming . . . Bill to you unless you want to be all on your dignity. I'm afraid I've forgotten what you said your names were. I'm sorry."

The two girls reintroduced themselves, and then Avril took up the cudgels again with:

"Please, you must listen to me, Bill. If you had not rescued Ann and me like you did, then we should have gone to the police in Keswick this morning. When we got back to the farm yesterday, Ann's father comes back from working with the rescue party. Then he tells us about the man who was missing. . . *and* about the missing diamonds. If you don't believe me . . . then wait for Miss Pringle and Miss Armstrong. They got all the newspapers I bring from Keswick, and the story is printed in each one of them. I tell you we speak the truth only."

Bill nodded, his brow furrowed in a deep frown.

"Well, I'm in a real jam now," he admitted. "Listen, what about these two . . . er . . . Miss Pringle and Miss Armstrong. There were two women came up the valley . . . about an hour before you did. As a matter of fact if they hadn't come up I think I'd have collared Felix by now. They came up, nattering away, and they scared him out of the patch of bracken where he was hiding. I'd marked the spot from a lookout I've found up the fellside. When I crept down, he'd gone. I went back . . . and then as I saw you finish with the sheep I also saw him moving through the bracken towards you. I think he must have got the scent of the meat."

"Those two women," Ann said soberly, "saw us with you yesterday. And *they* think you are the missing plane-man, don't they, Avril?"

"Yes, and they were watching when your lion came," Avril said. "We both see the sun shining on the lenses of their glasses . . . how do you call them, Ann? Not opera-glasses."

"Field-glasses," Ann suggested, and Avril nodded her thanks.

"That is it. Field-glasses! They watch us through these field-glasses from the crags up there," and she

pointed dramatically to the rugged outline of the
Tingle Crags.

Bill heaved himself round and looked. There was
no glint of sun on field-glass lens now, but he gave a
little grunt of dismay as he realised that from such a
short distance, good glasses would show up details
quite clearly.

"If they *were* watching us, it's ten to one they'll
have seen everything. They might even have seen
Felix. If he ran through the bracken and up on to the
rocks . . . the game is up. They'd see him for certain.
Oh, lor', what luck!"

Ann held out the packet of sandwiches, and for a
minute or so there was no more conversation. They
ate and thought, and the only sounds were those made
by the little rills which joined nearby to make the first
beginnings of the stream which ran through the
Brackendale farmyard.

High above, a raven flapped heavily across the valley,
croaking dismally. Shep and Nell sat bolt upright,
heads moving expectantly as first one, then another of
the trio took a sandwich and ate it. The sheep-dogs
merely looked, and hoped. It was Avril who finally
broke a sandwich in two pieces and tossed a half to
each dog. That seemed to break the gloomy spell, for
Bill asked:

"What sort of persons are these two women? I
mean . . . do you think we could persuade them not to
talk? If I could get just twenty-four hours I'd be all
right. Felix would be all right if that was a decent-

sized piece of meat you chucked to him, he . . ."

"There was ten pounds of it," Ann broke in.

"Hm. Well, that'd take the edge off his appetite," Bill agreed. "He'll still be hungry, for he won't have eaten since he escaped; but he won't be so ravenous that he'd attack anyone. If I could tempt him with some more meat to-morrow . . . I'd get him, I know I would."

"We might be able to bring some more meat," Ann said, but there was doubt in her voice as she went on: "Whether we could persuade Miss Pringle and her friend to keep mum is another matter."

"They would insist on talking," Avril said emphatically. "Ann, do you not remember Miss Armstrong, when she talk about the chance of getting the reward? She look to me like a . . . how do you say it? . . . someone who is looking at a lot of money. A miser? Is that the word? Someone who gloats over money."

"Miser is the word," Bill said gloomily. "And these women are like that, are they? If . . . here, but what reward are you talking about?"

"For the recovery of the diamonds," Ann said.

"Five thousand pounds," Avril said, her eyes shining with excitement. "That is what someone will give if the diamonds are brought back safely."

"Five thousand! Oh, lor'!" and Bill groaned. "Then that's it. If these women think I'm the chap from the plane you won't see their heels for dust."

Avril frowned, then said:

"Pardon! This is a new expression. We shall *not see their heels for dust*? What does that mean?"

"It means," Bill said grimly, "that they'll be in such a confounded hurry to get to the police, to say they've seen me, that they'll go as quick as their legs will carry them. If they're going quickly . . . they raise a dust, see?"

"Ah, yes," and Avril smiled and nodded. To Ann she said. "It is better to come to England to learn English . . . than to study books, Ann. There is so many things I hear which are not in books. I learn . . . oh, pardon, Bill. I am forgetting that we are in trouble."

"You aren't in trouble. Only me," Bill assured her.

"No . . . no, Bill," Avril insisted. "I say *we* are in trouble, for Ann and I have said we shall help you. You help us very much yesterday. So . . . we shall help you. That is good, eh?"

"It would be fine—if I knew *how* you could help me!" Bill agreed, not very hopefully.

"Well, first we shall think," Avril said brightly, "and . . .!" She stopped then, for the two dogs had suddenly ceased watching. Once again they had turned, ears cocked. Thinking of Felix, Ann, Avril and Bill turned to look in the same direction, beyond the bracken. After a moment all three groaned in chorus.

Coming down the track, and obviously in a hurry, were two women, Miss Pringle and Miss Armstrong.

"On their way to the nearest police station," Bill

said grimly. "They're not hurrying like that for fun. Cor, look at 'em. Hm! Well, Felix, I did my best, and if I hadn't bust up this ankle I might still have saved you; but if we get a crowd of coppers up here, looking for a jewel thief . . . it'll be the end of you."

"Wait a minute," Ann said, "I think I've got an idea."

"Now we shall be all right, Bill," Avril said. "When Ann has an idea . . . then everything will be happy. No . . . that is not right. Every*one* will be happy. We . . . oh!" The smile faded from her face as Ann, standing up, began waving a hand as she shouted:

"Miss Pringle . . . Miss Pringle . . . yo-oh."

The hurrying figures stopped as abruptly as if they had walked into a stone wall. They were obviously puzzled at the sight of Ann, apparently alone. Bill and Avril were still seated, and hidden by the bracken.

"Where's the French girl?" Miss Pringle shouted. "Has something happened?"

"Yes, can you come here?" Ann shouted back. "We need your help."

There was no more hesitation. Miss Pringle led the way with her friend hard on her heels.

"What are you going to say?" Avril asked anxiously.

"It all depends on them," Ann whispered. "I'm going to try and get them on our side."

CHAPTER V

A BATTLE OF WITS

When Miss Pringle rounded the edge of the bracken path and saw Avril and Bill, she stopped so abruptly that Miss Armstrong walked straight into her. In the next few moments Ann felt she could read the thoughts of the two women almost as if they were printed in large letters on a huge sheet of paper.

Two pairs of eyes took in all the details: Bill's bandaged hand, his ankle swathed in wet cloth, the open rucksacks, the flasks and the cups.

For perhaps ten seconds no one spoke. Shep went up to Miss Armstrong and nuzzled her hand, an act which brought a little squeak of protest and gave Ann an excuse for breaking the silence with a command to her dog.

"Shep . . . come here, that's a good boy."

Then Bill spoke.

"Good afternoon, ladies. I must apologise for not rising, but as you can see I've had a little tumble . . . and ricked my ankle."

"Oh . . . er . . . good afternoon," Miss Pringle said, and turned to Ann appealingly. Ann did what was expected of her at once.

"This is Mr. Leaming," she said, indicating Bill, and with another wave of the hand went on: "Miss Pringle and Miss Armstrong."

"Mr. *Leaming!*" Miss Pringle had a question in her voice as she repeated Bill's name. "Leaming. Hm!"

Bill, with his back to the wall, and certain his secret would soon be out, sat bolt upright as he said:

"By the way you say my name, Ma'am, it almost sounds as if you think you know me. If you do, I must apologise, for I cannot recollect meeting you before."

"Oh . . . I'm sorry," Miss Pringle hurriedly apologised. "No . . . I . . . don't think we have met. It was the name. For some reason another name came into my mind."

Then Avril laughed, a mischievous laugh.

"I know . . . I know," she said, and wagging a finger in Bill's direction she went on: "Miss Pringle thinks you should have said your name was Sissons."

Both Miss Pringle and Miss Armstrong gasped at that, while Bill frowned and shrugged.

"Sissons? Why in the name of goodness should I have a name like that?"

"You do not know, of course," Avril chuckled, and winking at Miss Pringle and the horrified Miss Armstrong, went on: "In the newspapers this morning there is a long story of an aeroplane which crashed in the mountains . . . over the ridge."

Bill nodded. "I've seen the wreckage of the plane," he admitted.

"But perhaps you did not know that one of the passengers ... by name Mr. Sissons, is missing, and with him is a packet of jewels ..."

"Diamonds," Miss Pringle could not prevent herself from correcting Avril.

"So ... diamonds," Avril agreed. "I think that Miss Pringle and Miss Armstrong maybe imagine that you are Mr. Sissons and have the diamonds. Yes?" and she turned, an impish gleam in her eyes, to look across at the two schoolteachers.

In that moment Ann could have hugged her friend until she squeezed the breath from her lungs. It was just like the French girl to snatch at a chance like this and turn the tables.

Miss Pringle coughed. Miss Armstrong was chewing nervously at her lower lip. Bill, snatching at a straw, chuckled most convincingly and said :

"Diamonds! No wonder you ladies gave me a pretty hard stare when you saw me. I'm sorry if I disappointed you ... but I'm afraid I'm nothing like so romantic a person as a diamond thief."

"No?" There was a hard note in Miss Pringle's voice now. She had recovered her self-possession, and was not convinced. "Well, as long as the subject has been brought up, I'm going to admit that Miss Armstrong and I did think you might be the missing man. We saw you yesterday ... crawling round this very patch of bracken."

"Oh! Hm! Well, well." Bill, also, was not going to give in without a fight. "I hope you weren't spying on me. If you were I'm afraid you must be rather disappointed."

"There was no question of spying," Miss Pringle said stiffly. "We just happened to be on Tingle Crags, and viewing the valley with the aid of field-glasses. Naturally, seeing a man crawling round, and then into, a patch of bracken, we were interested. Later, when we heard that a man from the crashed plane was missing . . . we wondered."

"I am sorry you were disappointed," Bill said.

There followed another long silence, then Miss Pringle said:

"If you won't think me rude," she said, "might I ask what you were looking for in the bracken? You see, we were on Tingle Crags just now . . . and we saw the little incident, when you fell."

Bill had no ready answer for that; but by this time Ann could step into the breach.

"I know you must be very puzzled, Miss Pringle, and you too, Miss Armstrong, and I have a confession to make."

"Ah!" That was from Miss Armstrong. Miss Pringle merely stared and waited.

"You said yesterday evening that you had seen a man, and you asked if either Avril or I had seen him," Ann said quietly.

"I know," Miss Pringle was nodding significantly. "And Avril dropped her coffee cup. It was very clever, my dear. It provided a little diversion, and allowed you to leave the dining-room without anyone appearing to notice that you had not answered our question as to whether or not you had seen a man."

"Well, you can have the answer now," Ann said, smiling pleasantly. "We weren't intending to be rude. As it happened Mr. Leaming helped Avril and me yesterday. We had an accident which could have been serious if he had not come along. In return he asked us if we would like to help him. We agreed to do anything we could . . . and we were absolutely amazed when he told us what he was doing in our valley."

She turned and gave an apologetic shrug as she heard Bill Leaming draw in a swift breath.

"I know I promised to keep your secret," she said quietly, "but I think I must tell Miss Pringle and Miss Armstrong, otherwise they will go on thinking that you are the man who stole the diamonds. Miss Pringle . . ."

Miss Pringle nodded. She was waiting.

"You may find this hard to believe, Miss Pringle," Ann went on, "but it *is* true. Mr. Leaming believes there is a *big cat* in the bracken. He belongs to a circus, and he is hoping to take the big cat away with him. It will help him in his circus act."

Miss Armstrong looked at her friend, as if sure that such a story would never, never be accepted. She was right. There was a pitying little smile on Miss Pringle's face when she said:

"Ann, you surely do not except me to believe that?"

"Ma'm'selle!" Avril said eagerly. "Do you not know the old saying that truth is often stranger than fiction? I say . . ."

"I know the saying you mention," Miss Pringle said coldly, "but I am reluctant to believe Ann's story. No one is ever going to convince me that a man from a circus would come out here looking for a big cat. I'll tell you something . . . you know, I have been walking the Lake District fells for many years. I have read almost every book ever written about them . . . and I have no recollection of ever seeing in print a word about wild cats. Certainly not these days!"

"But I am here, Ma'am, as this girl says, to catch a big cat," Bill Leaming insisted. "No one but you has mentioned *wild* cats. I am here to find a tame *big cat*. I don't know why you doubt my word."

"You don't. Then I will tell you," and for a moment Miss Pringle's mouth closed into a thin line reminiscent of a sprung trap. "I don't believe the story, and I do not believe your name is Leaming. Joyce, I think we'll go."

"Wait!" There was an iron ring in Bill Leaming's voice. "If you are thinking of going to the police with news that the man they are looking for is in this valley, I beg of you to think again. I am *not* the diamond thief . . . and if you will give me two days, three at the most, I will prove it."

Miss Pringle shook her head, and again there was the pitying smile on her face.

"Mr. *Leaming*, in the past you may have dealt with

people who would believe any cock and bull story you
cared to think up. You may have been able to help
Ann and her friend . . . and got their sympathies, but
if I think it is my duty to inform the police that there
is a man in Brackendale valley, behaving in a queer
way . . . a man who does not want his whereabouts
made known . . . I shall inform them. If you want to
come down to the village now, and establish your
identity with the police . . . my friend and I will be
very glad to help you down."

Bill tapped with the tips of his fingers on a stone
for a moment or so, then shook his head.

"I'm sorry," he said, "but I've got to stay up here.
If you wish to go to the police that is your business and
I can't stop you."

Miss Pringle hesitated for a moment, then turning
on her heels started to walk towards the track again,
Miss Armstrong hurriedly falling in step with her.
Ann looked at Avril, then at Bill. For a moment it
seemed as if she might run after the two women, but
changing her mind sat down and with her elbows
on her knees cupped her chin in her hands.

"That's how I feel," Bill said. "Anyway, thanks a
lot for trying. I suppose we can't blame Miss Pringle
and her friend for deciding to inform the police. But
if the police come up here, and get one glimpse of
Felix, that'll be the end."

"And they will come up, surely," Avril said. "After
all . . . they search for a man who steals diamonds."

"Here, wait a minute," Ann said, and now she

was nibbling gently at a thumb nail. "I've had an idea. We might not gain anything . . . but we can't lose."

Bill Leaming tapped the butt of a cigarette on the back of his left hand, felt for his matches and waited. Ann had a faraway look in her eyes, which suggested she was weighing-up the chances of succeeding with the idea she had just had. Avril was also watching and waiting.

"If you stay up here," Ann said quietly, "you won't be able to do anything for at least a day, maybe two days, will you? Your ankle is swelling pretty badly, even with the cold compress on it."

Bill nodded glumly. The ricked ankle seemed about the last straw.

"Tell you what, then," Ann said, and now there was a growing note of excitement in her voice. "Suppose you come down to the farm. We have a spare bedroom, and Father won't mind when he knows you've had an accident. We . . ."

"Wait, wait," Bill urged. "What about Felix?"

"Avril and I would come up again with more meat . . . and hope your *big cat* will . . ."

"Oh, the *big* cat," Avril gurgled. "I think that is so funny. You tell the truth and neither Miss Pringle nor Miss Armstrong will even sniff at it. I am . . . oh, pardon, I am rude. I interrupt."

"As long as you can't possibly go after Felix until your ankle is better you might as well be comfortable down at our place," Ann urged. "If you come down

... well, we can keep an eye open for any policeman ...
or policemen. They might send for help from Keswick.
When we see them ... we call them into the farm and
introduce you. They'll realise at once you are not the
missing man—and so there will be no hunt in our
valley. Don't you think it's a good idea?"

For a moment there was silence save for the babble
of the stream and the soft panting of the two sheep-
dogs. Then a little smile started at the corners of Bill's
mouth and spread quickly until his face was one
huge grin. Avril had clasped her hands in an ecstasy
of joy. She rocked backwards and forwards, her lower
lip clenched between her teeth so that she would not
go off into a bout of uncontrollable laughter.

"You know, Ann," Bill said, "I'm beginning to
think you are a most extraordinary girl. You've got
brains, plenty of 'em, and you know how to use them.
There's going to be two very startled, and sheepish
ladies at your house when I walk in. There's only
one thing that worries me ... and that's the feeding
of Felix. It's putting you girls to a lot of trouble."

"Do not worry," Avril urged. "I am on holiday ...
and I enjoy this very much. It is adventure. Think
what I shall be able to tell my friends when I go back
to Paris. To-morrow, when Ann carries the next lot
of beef up here, I shall carry my camera. Then we shall
have pictures of this *big cat*. I shall laugh every time
I hear those two words." Striking a pose to represent
the dignified, somewhat scornful Miss Pringle, Avril
said, withering sarcasm in her voice: " 'I have read

every book written about the English Lake District, and nowhere does it say anything about wild cats.' So . . . she does not believe. Yet no one speaks of *wild* cats, only of a *big cat*."

Ann removed the wet bandage from about Bill's ankle, pursed her lips at sight of the swelling, and suggested he should hobble to the edge of the stream and sit with his foot in the water.

"I'll go back home and see if either Father or Thomas will come up with the mare. I imagine we can get her to within three or four hundred yards of here. I'll bring a couple of walking sticks, and we ought to be able to get you home without much trouble."

"I'm not going to try and say, 'thank you', Ann," Bill said quietly. "Perhaps you can guess how I feel."

"We do this sort of thing often," Ann assured him. "Don't forget . . . there are lots of people wander round these hills, and accidents do happen. After all, Father and Thomas wouldn't be members of the mountain rescue team if people didn't get into difficulties now and then. I'm afraid I'll be about an hour. While I'm away you can be telling Avril how to tackle the feeding of Felix correctly."

It was just an hour before she got back. Her father was with her, and though they had not managed to get their mare as close as Ann had suggested, the journey down to her was not too troublesome. With Mr. Birkett on one side, Ann on the other, and Avril carrying the two rucksacks, they got down to the mare, and the rest was easy.

Answering Mr. Birkett's question about sending word to where he was staying, Bill managed an easy laugh as he explained:

"As a matter of fact, Mr. Birkett, I'm not booked in anywhere, so no one is going to be worrying about me. Your daughter seemed to think there might be a spare bedroom at your house. If . . ."

"Oh yes; there's no question of bundling you off anywhere," Ann's father assured him. "You can stay with us as long as you like . . . providing you can put up with Ann's cooking. I'm used to it and it doesn't worry me. Anyway, her mother will be back in a few days."

"Daddy! I shall never speak to you again," Ann pouted, pretending to be angry. "You know very well I can cook. I'll tell you this; Mr. Leaming thought my coffee was so good he was sure Avril must have made it . . . she being French."

When they got down to the farm Mr. Birkett lent Bill a pair of trousers while the rent in the knee of the pair he had damaged was repaired. Avril did the sewing while Ann prepared afternoon tea, for it was now almost four o'clock. Mr. Birkett and Thomas had seen nothing of either Miss Pringle or Miss Armstrong, and thought they must still be out on the fells.

The first intimation they were not out tramping was when a police car drew up in the farmyard about four-thirty. A uniformed constable got out and opening the rear door helped out Miss Pringle and Miss Armstrong. Ann's father, imagining there had been an accident, hurried over from where he had been feeding the pigs.

"Now, Inspector, what's been happening? You haven't arrested my two guests, have you?" By this time he had noted that neither woman showed signs of having been in an accident.

Inspector Millom smiled, and nodding to the two constables and a sergeant who had also got out of the big car, indicated with a wave of his hand that they could move on up the valley. With the sergeant in the lead the constables started for the track leading up Brackendale to Tingle Crags.

The inspector turned to Mr. Birkett saying:

"No, we haven't arrested the two ladies; far from it. As a matter of fact they came down to the village with information. It looks as if they might have got a line on the missing man. The man from the crashed plane."

"They have? Well I'll be blowed," Mr. Birkett said, and turned a beaming face on his two guests. "Well, that's a caution if you like. And I'm proud of you. Here we have the police, and local men, spending hours and hours searching everywhere, in what we think are the likeliest places, and it's left to two lady visitors to find the chap."

"It's often the case," the inspector said. "We all think we know the mountains, but some of the people who come up here on holiday can still show us a thing or two. Anyway, I won't dally. If we get hold of this chap we'll call in on our way back. He'll have been without food and drink since the crash so he'll need something."

"The kettle's always on," Mr. Birkett assured him, "I'll expect you when . . . here, wait a minute. Are you going up the valley? Up Brackendale?"

"He's somewhere near the first big patch of bracken," the inspector said, "and he can't get away. He's had a tumble down a scree and . . . what's the matter?"

"Matter?" Mr. Birkett looked from the inspector to Miss Pringle, and then to Miss Armstrong. "Look, my daughter and her friend have been up there . . . and Ann came down for me, about an hour ago. We've just brought a chap down. *He's got a ricked ankle and a bandaged hand.*"

"That's him," Miss Pringle said, but she was now beginning to look a little flustered. "He said his name was Leaming."

"Leaming! It's the same fellow. You'd better call your men back, Inspector. Unless I'm mistaken your man is sitting in my front room at this very moment," Mr. Birkett said. "And now I come to think of it . . . he *could* be the missing man. I asked him where he'd been staying . . . y'know, so I could get word to them, and then they wouldn't be reporting him missing. He just laughed and said he had not booked in at any hotel, so I needn't worry. And so far as I was concerned, that was that."

"Hm. Sounds suspicious," the inspector agreed, and calling his sergeant brought him and the constables back to the farmyard at the double. To the con-

stables he said: "You lads can make yourselves comfortable for a few minutes. Have a smoke if you like.
Sergeant, you'll come with me. Now, Mr. Birkett, if
you'll lead the way we'll see who this chap is."

Ann's father rubbed his chin thoughtfully for a
moment, then chuckled as he said:

"This is going to be a bit of a mix-up, Miss Pringle,
if it works out as you think. You tell the police,
but I bring the chap in. Who gets the reward, if he is
the fellow from the plane? Anyway, I never did count
my chickens before they were hatched. Come on in,
and we'll get it over with."

A minute later he pushed open the dining-room door
and led the way in. The sun was pouring through
the leaded window, showing up the snow-white
table-cloth, and winking on the tea-cups. There was a
fine spread of home-made cakes and scones, a small
bowl of jam and, another of the Lake District's delica-
cies, rum butter. Bill Leaming was making the most
of it, with his injured leg resting on a fat cushion
placed on a stool. Conversation ceased as the Inspector
came forward, the Sergeant at his side.

"Good afternoon, sir," the inspector said gravely.
"Sorry to butt in like this. Could I have a few words
with you?"

"With pleasure," Bill said, smiling. "Do you mind
if I don't stand? I've bust up my ankle, and . . ."

"No, no, stay where you are, sir" the inspector said
politely. "Won't take more than a minute or so, anyway. I'll come straight to the point. I wonder if you

are aware that a man is missing from the plane which crash-landed on the far side of Brackendale the night before last?"

"These two young ladies told me," Bill said, indicating Ann and Avril.

"They probably told you that the missing man took with him a satchel containing precious stones."

"That's right," Bill agreed.

"Then you'll understand why I must ask you some questions," the inspector said. "We have to make a routine check of everyone in the area, so if you will give my sergeant some details . . . name, where you came from, where you were going, your permanent address, profession, etc., I'll be very glad."

In the next minute or so both Ann and Avril had the feeling that a net was closing around Bill. Both inspector and sergeant raised their eyebrows when Bill gave his profession as lion-tamer. When he admitted that he had no luggage with him, and that he left the circus five days previously, and had been in the Brackendale valley during the pass forty-eight hours, the eyebrows were raised even higher.

Finally, when Bill slowly shook his head when asked why he was in the Brackendale valley, the inspector pursed his lips and said:

"I think we'd better take you into Keswick, Mr. Leaming; and have that ankle seen by a doctor. You never know . . . there may be a bone or bones broken. We'll get a doctor to give it a check-over."

Bill shrugged, and smiled grimly.

"In other words, Inspector, you don't quite believe me, and want me where you can keep an eye on me, eh?"

"We've got our duty to do, sir," the inspector said, "as I am sure you will appreciate. After all, most people who come here for walking or climbing, bring some luggage with them, if it is only a rucksack. You won't tell us why you were hanging about the Brackendale valley . . . so. . . ."

"I can see your point," Bill said, nodding, "but . . . I give you my word I shall not try to run away. After all . . . my damaged ankle should be a pretty good insurance against me vanishing, shouldn't it? I don't want to go into Keswick. And I give you my word that I'll be able to explain everything in a day or so."

"I'm afraid I have my orders, sir," the inspector said. "I have to bring in anyone who cannot satisfy me as to why they are in the area. At the moment I'm not completely satisfied with your story."

"I was afraid you wouldn't be," Bill grinned ruefully, as he eased his injured ankle off the cushion. "Anyway, I won't be hard on you later on when you offer me your apologies. Sorry I have to go, Ann, and you, Avril. When I come back I hope we'll be able to finish the story I was in the middle of, eh?" and his raised eyebrows asked the question he dare not put into words: would they try and feed Felix, and keep the cougar quiet, until he got back?

The sergeant helped Bill out to the car. Mr. Birkett followed with the inspector, leaving the two girls alone with Miss Pringle and Miss Armstrong.

Ann looked at their two guests, both were a little pale. Angry words boiled to the tip of her tongue, but she kept them in check. After all, they were paying guests at Brackendale Farm, and she had to be polite to them.

Avril, however, had no intention of keeping quiet. Putting her clenched fists on the edge of the table she leaned forward and said:

"Well, I hope you are both happy, now that you have ruined Mr. Bill. It will be a most unhappy day for *you* . . . when he comes back and you see that you were so completely wrong. It will be too late then, for the damage will have been done and he will be ruined, completely ruined."

" I don't know what you are talking about," Miss Pringle said coldly. "If he is innocent . . . he will be released, and that will be that."

"No . . . no, no! no!" Avril's eyes were flashing, and when Ann laid a restraining hand on her friend's arm, the French girl put it gently away. "Sometimes it is said, 'two wrongs do not make a right.' Well, I am perhaps wrong in saying this thing to your guests, Ann ; but I see that you cannot speak. It would be rude for you. For me . . . well, I too am a guest. So I can speak. Miss Pringle, and Miss Armstrong . . . I shall tell you why this Mr. Bill was in the valley. Then you will see how wicked you have been to bring in the police. You . . ."

"Avril," Ann said urgently, "please . . . we promised not to say anything. It is a secret and . . ."

For a moment the French girl hesitated, then she

turned and wagged a finger almost under Ann's nose, saying:

"Ann, there is an English proverb which says: ' A stitch in time saves nine.' If we put in a stitch now . . . we save Bill. It is better that I speak, then these two ladies can see what they have done. They think there is a reward . . . ooh, la la, the reward is shame, for they have ruined a good man. Miss Pringle . . . ."

CHAPTER VI

FOUR TO FEED FELIX

ANN'S FATHER came into the house and Avril choked back the flood of words.

"Lion-tamer, he said he was," Mr. Birkett chuckled, walking into the room and beginning to pour himself a cup of tea. "Well, I've met some queer folks in and around Brackendale, but I never met a chap before who said he was a lion-tamer. And, you know, he said it as if he expected us to believe him."

Ann caught at Avril's wrist as she felt the French girl stiffen, as if there and then she was going to blurt out the truth about Bill Leaming. Miss Pringle and Miss Armstrong stayed only for a few moments, then excused themselves and went to their rooms.

"I'm keeping the rest of the sheep down here until to-morrow," Ann's father said, finishing his cup of tea. "Then if you and Avril could take them up . . . we'd know they'd be well out of the valley for when the Hound Trail starts. If we can get them over the Long Face fell, they're not likely to stray back before to-morrow night, and it won't matter then. How did you like being a shepherd, Avril? Easy, isn't it?"

Avril somehow managed a convincing smile.

"I like it very much, Mr. Birkett. And to-morrow I

shall love to take the others up the valley. Now . . . I think I go and have a bath. I shall ride into Keswick afterwards. Or, no, maybe I ride into Keswick now . . . I shall need a bath afterwards, for it is hot work riding."

"I shouldn't go into Keswick now," Ann's father protested. "What is it you want? I'm going into the village later on, and I'll get Sam Yealand to . . ."

"Thank you, thank you," Avril said, smiling, "but this Sam cannot get for me quite the thing I want. I am not being ungrateful, I hope."

"No, no, just do what you like, my dear," Ann's father said, feeling for his pipe. "We want you to enjoy yourself as much as possible. I'm only sorry I haven't an excuse for going into Keswick myself, or I'd have taken you in."

"Perhaps you could borrow a bike, Ann," Mr. Birkett said, "and go in with Avril. Oh, but I forgot, there's dinner to prepare for the two ladies. Anyway, don't go tiring yourself too much, Avril. This is only your second day, y'know. There's still plenty of time for doing things. Anyway, I must leave you and give Thomas a hand."

The moment he was out of the house Ann looked at her friend, shrugged, and said:

"Well?"

"Ann," Avril said quietly. "I am your guest. Tell me if I am behaving badly. I wish to go into Keswick to buy more meat for Felix; but first I think we should tell these two ladies the truth."

"Why? What good is it going to do?" Ann asked.

"I tell you," Avril said urgently. "I think they will help."

"You have a hope," Ann said, shaking her head doubtfully.

"I have lots of hope," Avril insisted. "These two ladies ... they are very ... how do you say it ... good? No, that is not the word. They wish to do the right thing. Yes. That is it. So ... we tell them they have injured our friend Mr. Bill. Then they will be anxious to help him."

"I can't see it," Ann shook her head again.

"Then wait and see. Come, there is not time to lose. We go and beard the lion in his den." She laughed happily. "That is good proverb this time, eh? I learn many English proverbs. Do not look so troubled, Ann. They will not put the blame on you. If they are angry they will say: 'Ah, these French ... they are barbarians.' But I hope they will not be angry."

Somewhat reluctantly, Ann led the way up the stairs and tapped on the door of Miss Pringle's room. The murmur of conversation ceased, and then Miss Pringle called: "Come in."

When she saw Avril following on Ann's heels her smile faded and a frosty look came into her eyes.

"Avril would like to speak to you," Ann said.

"I come to apologise," Avril said breezily. "I have too many bad manners and I use them too much. Please, forgive me. I have something to tell you, and when you have listened, maybe you will not be too angry, no?"

"We were all rather upset, I think, weren't we, Jean?" Miss Armstrong said, shooting a quick glance at Miss Pringle, as if half-afraid Avril's apology might not be accepted.

Avril did not give Miss Pringle time to say anything, but went on:

"You maybe think, like the policeman, that Mr. Bill tells a lie when he says he is a lion-tamer. Ann and I know that he tells the truth . . . for we *have seen his lion!* It is in the valley . . . near where you saw us this noon."

Miss Pringle's brow furrowed into a frown. Miss Armstrong's mouth opened into a round O, but no sound came forth.

"This Mr. Bill lose a lion . . . a mountain lion, a few days ago," Avril said, and went on quickly explaining the whole story, coming to the point where Bill Leaming had been instrumental in getting her and Ann out of the crevice into which they had fallen.

"He cannot tell the policeman he is here to catch a lion," Avril went on, "for then there will be a hunt; Felix will be shot, and Mr. Bill is ruined."

"Oh dear," Miss Armstrong murmured, deep concern in her voice.

"I say to Ann," Avril went on, her eyes shining, "I say . . . once Miss Pringle and Miss Armstrong know the truth then they will want to help. I say . . . these two ladies are . . . how do you put it? . . . are . . . *real* ladies, that is it: real ladies. They will not see a man like Mr. Bill ruined. They will help."

"Help!" Miss Pringle said, "I'm afraid I cannot see how we could possibly help. After all . . ."

"It is simple," Avril went on like a mountain stream in flood. "All we have to do is take beef up to feed the mountain lion Felix, . . . and he keeps quiet and happy until Mr. Bill returns to capture him."

"We took a ten pound piece of beef up this morning," Ann explained. "Mr. Leaming insists that Felix is really quite tame. He is not a forest-bred lion at all. He was born in captivity."

"That doesn't mean a thing," Miss Pringle said doubtfully. "I have heard of lions and tigers born in captivity, and kept as pets; but once they were full-grown they became dangerous."

"But this Felix, he came quite near to us for the meat," Avril said, "and you can see neither Ann nor I are hurt one little scratch."

"We ought to do something, Jean dear," Miss Armstrong whispered. "After all . . . I suppose if we had not informed the police the man would still be at liberty, wouldn't he?"

"Yes, I suppose he would," Miss Pringle admitted grudgingly, then, and her eyes lit up. "But . . . have you forgotten that there is to be a Hound Trail to-morrow? The valley will be alive with dogs . . . and there will be men going up there, too, laying the trail. You can't possibly let them go on with the Hound Trail, without warning them there is a wild animal roaming about."

There was a short pause. Ann had temporarily

forgotten the forthcoming Hound Trails, and what Miss Pringle said was true enough. Two men would walk up one side of the valley, cross it at the top, and come down the other side. They would drag a bag of aniseed the whole way, thus laying a trail for the hounds. When they were back at Brackendale farm the hounds competing in the first event would be released and, watched by excited spectators, would follow the scent round the whole course. The risk of a clash between hounds and the cougar was obvious.

"I suppose," said Ann, after a long pause, "if Felix had been very well-fed he might sleep through it all. Mr. Leaming did say he usually slept after a feed."

"But suppose he didn't," Miss Armstrong suggested timidly. "Suppose he jumped out on the men who were laying the aniseed trail. Have you thought about that?"

"Or even if he did not attack the men . . . he might attack the dogs. Or the dogs might get his scent and attack him." Miss Pringle shook her head soberly as she added: "I really do think it is our duty to warn the people, don't you? If we don't, I'm sure we shall be taking a dreadful risk."

Avril, however, was not to be put off.

"I take a big risk, Miss Pringle, when I tell you our secret. But I have said to myself—and I say it to Ann—these two ladies do not know they have done wrong to Mr. Bill. When they know they have made a mistake, then they will be very anxious to help. If Mr. Bill loses his Felix, then he loses his job. Do you not understand? He says his mountain lion will not attack anyone . . . so long as he is well-fed. I believe him. I believed you would like to help . . . but I think maybe, I make mistake."

"My dear young lady," Miss Pringle began, only to be interrupted by her friend, Miss Armstrong, who said coaxingly:

"Jean, maybe we could do something. I feel so dreadful about getting Mr. Leaming arrested. After all, if this . . . lion, is tame . . ."

"We have only *his* word for it," Miss Pringle reminded her acidly. "If this cougar clawed a man . . ."

"If he has a good meal," Ann said, "I believe he would not feel like attacking anyone. Anyway, I am sorry we troubled you, and . . ."

Miss Armstrong broke in. She was pale and agitated as she turned to her friend.

"Jean . . . we must do something. Look, Ann, at least we could help you get the meat. Could I run you into Keswick in my car?"

"Ah, Miss Armstrong, I knew *you* would help," and sweeping round the table Avril kissed the startled Miss Armstrong on both cheeks, then gave her a hug. "Now I know all will be well. Your car would save so much time . . . it is hard work to pedal to Keswick and back again."

"I think you are being very foolish, Joyce," Miss Pringle said, "but if you insist . . . I shall come with you."

"I shall come too," Avril announced. "I have been

to this shop for the meat already. If *I* buy it then you will not feel awkward, eh? I am French, and the man maybe thinks French girls eat a lot of meat. I buy ten pounds this morning . . . maybe I ought to buy more this time to make sure our mountain lion eats until he is sleepy."

She laughed, an infectious laugh which somehow melted the iciness from Miss Pringle's eyes. As she turned to leave the room Avril said:

"I shall be ready in—how does Thomas say it?— the waggle of a ram's tail? No. The wag of a lamb's tail. That is . . . quickly."

In the kitchen, with Avril sluicing face and hands at the sink, Ann said admiringly:

"Avril, you really are a marvel. I never thought you'd do it. Miss Pringle is a tough nut."

"I think Miss Pringle is nice," Avril spluttered from the depths of the towel. "When I finish with these two ladies I have them both as friendly as a sheep-dog. How do you say it? . . . eating out of my hands?"

"I doubt it."

"Ah, but you forget something, Ann," Avril insisted. "Miss Pringle and Miss Armstrong are schoolteachers, yes? They must all the time be dig . . . ni . . . So very dignified; but they are not fools. They look at the possible dangers, which is right. However, we shall have them carrying a great lump of English beef up the valley to Felix before we finish. I think it will do them good."

"I hope so," Ann murmured.

A few minutes later she watched the little car trundle down the rutty road towards the village. Miss Armstrong was at the wheel, Miss Pringle was in the back with Avril.

"Avril could talk a brass monkey into giving its nuts to her," Ann murmured, "but Miss Pringle is tougher than Miss Armstrong, a lot tougher."

Walking back into the kitchen she began preparations for the evening meal, but her thoughts were not on the food. She could not get out of her mind's eye a picture of what would be happening next day in the Brackendale valley.

The peace and the quiet would be gone from about noon onwards. Cars would arrive in a steady stream, bringing dogs and their owners, spectators, and the bookmakers, for there was always a lot of betting on the events. Hounds would be yapping, bookmakers would be shouting, car engines would be roaring as more and more people arrived, and struggled to get their vehicles into advantageous positions.

When the men laying the trail went off the crowd would watch them eagerly, to note every part of the course the hounds would have to take, and so perhaps guess which dog had the best chance of coming in first.

Thomas came in to ask Ann for something her father wanted, and she suddenly decided to ask his advice.

"Thomas, if you were laying the trail to-morrow, whereabouts would you take it? The last time they had Hound Trails here the big patch of bracken up the valley was much smaller than it is now, and they were able to keep the dogs out of it. If they want to keep them out of the bracken to-morrow they'll have to lay the trail over the foot of the screes, won't they?"

Thomas pondered for a moment then shook his head.

"They'll not take hounds over the screes, Ann," he assured her. " 'Twould be too hard on their paws. What they'll probably do is go right through the bracken. Them as is taking the aniseed bag will walk side by side, so they'll break a bit of a path for the hounds. The hounds'll get through right enough. I'm putting a shilling on Braystone Lassie for the first trail. She's got a nose as sharp as a knife. She don't miss nothing. Keen as mustard, she is."

Ann nodded her thanks, and was even more worried when Thomas was gone. She went to the front door and looked up the valley. The bracken stretched like a big carpet from scree to scree, and somewhere in it was Bill Leaming's cougar.

"And if they get his scent," she groaned, "the chances are they'll forget the aniseed, and then there'll be trouble."

She was so worried she allowed a pan of milk to boil over on the calor gas stove, and the smell of it was still in the kitchen when a squeal of brakes told of the return of the car from Keswick.

She confided her fears to Avril and the two school-teachers. To her surprise Miss Pringle said:

"Ann, if ever women get into politics in France, Avril will become the best Propaganda Minister the country has ever possessed. If anyone had told me that I could be persuaded to try and capture an escaped cougar, I would have dismissed them as completely mad."

"You . . . you mean you will help?" Ann could scarcely believe her ears.

"Avril has talked me into it," Miss Pringle agreed, smiling. "Mind you, don't think I'm going up the valley with a whip in one fist and a lasso in the other. My idea . . ."

"Miss Pringle has the wonderful idea, Ann," Avril burst in, her eyes shining. "She thinks that . . . oh, I am so sorry. I am being rude again. Excuse me, please."

"As I was saying," Miss Pringle went on, as if Avril had not uttered one word, "my idea is that we should make this mountain lion so sleepy that not even a score of yapping hounds would waken it. And it ought to be fairly simple. I don't know why we didn't think of it before."

Ann merely stared. A simple way of putting a mountain lion into a sleepy state was more than she could think of.

"Aspirins," Miss Pringle said, smiling. "After all, if we cannot sleep, what do we do? We take a couple of aspirins, and very soon we've drifted off."

"Ye—es," Ann agreed hesitantly. "But . . . how will you get Felix to take aspirins? If I take an aspirin I pop it into my mouth, drink a tumbler of water, and that is it."

"How do you give a child a nasty powder?" asked Miss Pringle. "You take a spoonful of jam, tip the powder on to it, mix it up . . . and because the child only sees the jam, and doesn't think there is a nasty powder mixed in it, the jam goes down and so does the powder."

Ann still frowned. It was a good idea giving a child a powder mixed with jam; but a hungry mountain lion was not exactly a child. Then the word "hungry" made her think.

"She understands," Avril shrilled, seeing the light dawning in Ann's eyes.

"In the meat?" Ann asked, and three heads nodded agreement.

"If we put a dozen aspirins in the meat . . . the lion gobbles it down, the aspirins add their weight to the sleep-inducing effects of a good meal, and we should have Mr. Leaming's mountain lion sleeping like a baby." And Miss Pringle beamed.

They discussed ways and means of getting the meat to Felix. There were sheep to be taken on to the fells in the morning, but that would not be a good time to put the mountain lion to sleep.

The sleeping "dose" would work best if given about an hour before the first of the Hound Trails began. It was decided that Miss Pringle and Avril should take a walk up the valley, carrying the meat with them, and put it in a likely spot about an hour or an hour and a quarter before the first batch of hounds were loosed. That, they thought, would give Felix time to have his meal and for the aspirins to do their work.

In the quiet of their bedroom under the eaves, Ann and Avril discussed the next day, and both felt happier. With Miss Pringle and Miss Armstrong on their side, there seemed much more chance of success.

"I tell you, Ann," Avril said a little boastfully, "I know the moment I see Miss Pringle that here is a woman with brains . . . and courage. You see how she thinks of a simple way of capturing Felix, eh?"

"Not capturing," Ann pointed out. "Putting him to sleep for the period of the Hound Trails. I think we ought to leave the capturing of Felix to Mr. Leaming."

"But I have had an idea," Avril insisted. "Felix will eat this great lump of beef. He will be ready for an after-lunch nap anyway, but with the aspirins . . . he will be sound, sound asleep. So . . . I think we take up one of the big nets which your papa has over one of his stacks of dried grass. It is a good idea, Ann, yes? What do you think?"

"Well," Ann yawned, "I suppose if Felix was very sound asleep you might get a net round him. But whether Daddy's hay nets are strong enough I wouldn't like to say."

"Ah yes," Avril insisted confidently. "But you forget that this Felix is a *tame* lion. Mr. Bill said so. When he feels he is in the net, he will give up. You shall see."

"All right, I hope so. I . . . oo-ooo-ooh! I'm tired.

Good night, and don't forget to say your prayers."

"Good night, Ann. I wish it was to-morrow. It is going to be one of my big days. Plenty of excitement. Maybe there will be pictures in the papers when we capture Felix. Won't everyone be surprised, eh? They . . . Ann . . . Ann."

Ann gave a little sigh, and hoped Avril would take it that she had drifted off to sleep. The French girl had been out of bed as early as Ann that morning, but she had *watched* while Ann milked the cows and put the gallons of creamy white through the cooler. She had chattered away while Ann fed the hens and collected the eggs. In Paris, Avril went to bed late and got up about half-past seven. Ann got up at six o'clock, and usually went to bed about half-past nine.

"Ah, so Ann is asleep already," Avril whispered, burrowing deeper into the huge feather pillow. "How I wish it was morning. I just know it will be a very wonderful day. M'sieur Felix, you can enjoy your last night in the open air. To-morrow . . . we shall hand you back to your master."

Up the valley, eyes glowing like minute green lamps as he crouched in the bracken, the cougar waited, every muscle tense. He was hungry; very hungry. In captivity he had regular meals. Since escaping he had eaten only one substantial piece of beef.

In the mountains where he might have been born had his mother not been made captive, he would have lived off deer. In such conditions a kill every three or four days would have been enough. A deer would provide a cougar with much more than a hundred pounds of beef, and the wild species is satisfied to eat every two or three days. Felix was different. In five days he had eaten only ten pounds of meat.

Crouched in the grass he was listening to the myriad sounds which his ears were picking up. A field-mouse was within a yard of him, yet the mountain lion wanted to be absolutely sure of a kill before whipping out his powerful right paw. Seven or eight times he had tried to catch a field-mouse, and each time he had missed by a hair's-breadth. He was not a skilled hunter.

Eyes closing until they were little more than green slits of living fire, he suddenly swept out his paw. The bracken crackled as green stems broke. The mouse gave a squeak and jumped. The paw thumped the earth where the little creature had been a split second before.

Every muscle quivering, the cougar waited, his eyes now round as moons. Then he nuzzled at his right forepaw, as if not yet sure whether he had made a kill or missed his aim. When he realised there was no mouse under his paw his eyes seemed to flame afresh. Lifting his head he gave a hoarse, coughing bark of anger and disappointment, then bounded away through the bracken.

Up on the fells sheep lifted their heads in amazement. Those that were cropping the thin grass stopped, suddenly alert. None of them had ever heard a sound like that which now echoed and re-echoed over the hills; but some age-old instinct seemed to tell them that it meant danger. Ewes called anxiously to their two and three-month-old lambs. There was a sudden increase in bleating, and Mr. Birkett's Herdwicks drew together in uneasy groups.

In the valley below, Felix vented his rage on a young rowan tree. He almost ran headlong into its slender trunk. Hissing in rage he reached up on his hind legs, his forepaws stretching up the trunk as far as they would go. Then he dug his claws deep and drew them down, tearing the smooth bark in a series of half-inch deep gashes.

Hunger was beginning to change Bill Leaming's Felix from a placid circus performer into a bad-tempered, hungry hunter. When he had vented some of his rage on the tree he stood for a moment or so, his tail swishing from side to side. Then he made the quiet night throb once more with his harsh, challenging bark. There was no answer, for the bleating of sheep on the higher reaches was silenced by the sound.

Felix lay down, purring in a bad-tempered fashion. When the first pale streaks of the false dawn lit up the sky in the east he was still there, kept awake by hunger. Nor had he moved when the real dawn came in, with every promise of another glorious summer day. Then, when the sun peeped over the distant hilltops he strode into the bracken. The fronds waved for a few moments, then were still.

In the quiet of the morning sounds carried far, and there came up to the hungry cougar the challenging crow of a rooster. His eyes flickered for a moment. A cow at Brackendale began to low. It was almost milking time. It was a new day; the day of the Hound Trails.

Lying just in the edge of the bracken Felix sulked. He was very hungry.

CHAPTER VII

MISS PRINGLE'S PLAN FAILS

ABOUT TEN o'clock Ann gathered the last of the sheep which had been dipped and started them on the track up the valley. Shep and Nell trotted soberly behind them. There was little to do when sheep were being taken back to the fells, for they were only too eager to go.

"We must keep a lookout when we get near the bracken," Ann said. "In fact I think we'll take the sheep on to the tops before we get to the place where we saw Felix, just in case he should be there again. I don't want to risk the dogs getting his scent."

"I wish we could have got something more powerful than aspirins," Avril said. "I think it would have been so much easier to give Felix his meat now . . . but of course, with aspirins, that would be no use. He would most likely waken again before the hounds finish charging up and down the valley."

"This is one time when I wish it could have rained hard, and brought a mist into the valley," Ann said. "Though the people who organise these Hound Trails don't always cancel them because of bad weather."

As they drew nearer the bracken they kept passing the field-glasses from one to the other, scanning the green carpet for a sign of the cougar, but there was not a sign of him.

The Herdwicks wanted to go up to the tops the usual way, but Ann used her dogs, and turned the flock before they reached the bracken. Once the sheep were going steadily up, the two girls halted and spent a quarter of an hour vainly trying to get some hint of where Felix was lying-up.

When they got back to the farm the first of the Hound Trail people were arriving. There was the starter, two judges and the two men who would lay the trail. A big mobile canteen followed the officials' car into the long meadow, and the first flurry of activity began as the caterer's assistants started to unload tables and prepare for the many snacks they hoped to serve later on when the crowds arrived.

In bygone days the farmer's wife would have been busy for a day or so before the Hound Trails, preparing a mountain of meat patties, slabs of cake and bread fingers. Several huge joints of meat would have been roasted, and girls from nearby farms would have been recruited to cut and butter bread and make sandwiches. None of this was necessary now, for the caterer's calor gas stoves were already burning, and he was busy filling his big urns with water.

Ann's father and Thomas were talking to the officials, apparently discussing the best route for the men who would lay the trail, and Ann heard a phrase which did not reassure her.

"You'll have to get through the bracken both going up and coming down again. It runs right up to the foot of the screes. We don't seem to be able to check it."

Through the bracken; just as Thomas had said the night before. If Felix was in the bracken, and not drugged, there would be trouble.

Miss Pringle and Miss Armstrong were waiting for the two girls, and the former was frowning a little, another bad sign.

"I've been thinking, Ann," she said. "What do we do if this mountain lion doesn't take the meat? I suppose it is possible that he might have gone right up the valley, or might not get the scent of it. It could be dangerous, then, couldn't it?"

"But we must hope that he *will* take the meat," Avril said brightly. "He took it from Ann and me, and that was a day ago. Surely he will be hungry again."

"I'm sure he will be hungry," Miss Pringle agreed, "but if he doesn't get the scent of the meat in time . . . well, he will still be hungry when the men who lay the trail go up through the bracken. Or, even if he doesn't attack them, he might attack the dogs. I understand, Ann, that some of these hounds are fairly valuable, aren't they?"

"Oh, heck, yes," Ann agreed. "There'd be a terrible row if some of them were injured . . . or killed."

"But you are not suggesting that we . . . that we let Mr. Bill down?" Avril could not conceal the anxiety she felt. "We must try. If Felix will not come for the meat . . . then we must think of something else. That is a good idea, yes?" and she turned appealingly to Ann, then to the two visitors.

"Joyce and I have discussed this," Miss Pringle said, "and while we want to help, we feel we should protect the men and the dogs. This is what we suggest. Avril and I will take the meat up. Joyce, who has a pair of powerful field-glasses, can go up the hill behind the farm. From there she will be able to watch us. So long as there is no signal from us, she can assume everything is going to plan. In other words, Felix has taken the meat. If he does not show up . . . then we wave a handkerchief. Joyce will come down to the farm, tell Ann, and then I think she ought to warn the Hound Trail officials that there is this . . . er . . . danger up the valley."

Avril turned and looked appealingly at Ann, as if pleading with her to think of some other way out. Ann, too, was worried. She wanted to help Bill Leaming; she did not want the cougar to be shot; but she could not get out of her thoughts what might happen if a hungry animal like Felix attacked the trail layers, or even the dogs.

Finally she nodded agreement.

"I'll put my boots on, Ann," Miss Pringle said, "and I'll be ready in a few minutes. I think we ought to be starting fairly soon. We must give the aspirins time to do their work."

Alone in the farm kitchen for the moment, Avril turned to Ann, a quiver in her voice as she said:

"Ann . . . Ann, you must think, quick. What shall we do if this Felix does not come for the meat? I am beginning to feel frightened for Mr. Bill. He helped us so much, and I think I should cry if we do not help him now. He is depending on us, you know."

"I know, I know," Ann agreed; "but I can't think what else we could do if Felix doesn't come for the meat. Anyway," she tried to shrug off the feeling of impending disaster, "Let's hope Felix will come. If he does, and if the aspirins work . . . maybe everything will work out all right."

Avril nodded miserably.

"This is one time, Ann, when I am afraid of that small word 'if'. If this, if that . . . I know that if anything goes wrong and our Felix is shot it will spoil the holiday completely."

"Better snatch a cup of coffee," Ann urged. "I'll make a sandwich for you. You won't be back for an hour at least, maybe longer than that."

Ten minutes later Miss Pringle and Avril left the back of the farm, so as not to attract the attention of Mr. Birkett, and began their trek up the valley. Avril carried the rucksack holding the lump of beef, in which the aspirins had been inserted.

Miss Armstrong fidgeted about for another half-hour, then left with her field-glasses for the rise from which she could look right up the valley, and see the spot where the previous day Ann and Avril had thrown the first lump of beef to Felix.

During the next forty minutes more and more people began to arrive, some in cars, some in shooting-brakes, and the quiet of Brackendale was gone. Men and women were walking about, exercising the beautiful Lake District hounds, and there was an unending chorus of shrill yaps and yelps, the roar of car engines, and now the shouting from two of the bookmakers who had set up their stands, and were trying to attract those who wanted to make bets on the dogs of their choice.

There were a few moments of quietness as men and women gathered to watch the two trail layers. They were youngish men, good walkers, who could go round the Brackendale valley at a rare pace, dragging behind them the bag soaked in aniseed. One or two of the hounds, getting a whiff of the aniseed strained at their leashes, and had to be dragged farther down the field.

In five minutes the trail layers were hidden by a fold in the ground, and except for a handful of people anxious to know exactly where the trail led, the rest of the spectators turned to chatting, or making sure of a snack at the mobile canteen.

Ann kept looking at her wrist-watch, and then towards the little rise where Miss Armstrong would be waiting.

"They say ' no news is good news '," she murmured

once, "but I'm wishing now we had arranged a signal to tell me that Felix had taken the meat. If I have to wait in suspense much longer I think I'll scream. I wonder what's happening up there!"

'Way up the valley nothing was happening. Avril and Miss Pringle walked at their best pace until they reached the fringe of the great patch of bracken. It was hot, and even though a gentle breeze was blowing in their faces, they were both perspiring by the time Avril took off the rucksack and began to unlace the top.

She pulled a little face as she drew out the lump of beef. It was wrapped in butcher's wrapping paper, but even that felt sticky. Holding the beef she turned to Miss Pringle and asked:

"Now, Miss Pringle?"

"Well, you know where the cougar came yesterday," was the immediate retort. "I suggest we lay it on the grass near the bracken, then go a short distance away and wait."

Avril stripped the paper from the meat, rolled it into a ball, and was about to put it into the rucksack again, and so avoid leaving any litter about; then had a thought.

"I shall throw this into the bracken," she said. "It must smell of beef, and maybe it will help bring Felix here."

She tossed the little ball of paper as far into the bracken as she could, then turned to follow Miss Pringle to a vantage spot some fifty yards away. As she mopped her damp face she looked round, hoping, half-expecting to see the bracken waving as it had waved the previous day when Felix had been making his way to the first ten pound piece of beef. Now a new piece of beef was there, but as yet there was no sign of the cougar.

There was hardly a sign of movement among the bracken fronds. The hot sun was killing the breeze, and it was the merest zephyr, blowing down the valley from the direction of Tingle Crags.

Up on the fells they could see a few sheep, grazing contentedly. They looked like little balls of dirty grey against the green. Occasionally the sound of bleating came faintly on the still air. It was a scene of perfect peace and quiet.

Apart from the distant baa-ing, and the buzz of insects, the only other sound was a low drone which was made by a large aircraft flying north at about ten thousand feet.

Miss Pringle looked at her watch, pursed her lips, then said:

"I think we should give the cougar twenty minutes at the most, Avril, don't you? If he hasn't come by then I'm sure we ought to take action."

"But why twenty minutes?" Avril asked anxiously. "Why not half an hour, forty minutes . . . maybe longer. After all, it is a long way to the valley top."

"I'm sure a hungry animal wouldn't take more than twenty minutes . . . probably a lot less, to come from the top of the valley," Miss Pringle said crisply.

"And don't forget, time is going on. It can't be so long, now, before the men who trail the aniseed bag start out. We must be sure no harm will befall them. Once they start out I fancy it will not be easy to stop them. If we told them about the cougar I doubt if they'd believe us."

Avril was silent, and for the next fifteen minutes she scanned the valley from scree edge on the south to scree edge on the north, and right across the bracken to the top of Tingle Crags in the west. A kestrel was quartering an area near the top of the valley, and twice it *stooped* as if about to make a kill, but each time it rose with swift winnowing wings just before it reached the rocks.

"Well," Miss Pringle broke the silence, "I really think we must signal to Miss Armstrong. Time is just racing along . . ."

"Please, Miss Pringle," Avril pleaded. "Maybe you could give Felix another few minutes. I am sure he will come."

Against her better judgment Miss Pringle agreed, but at the end of five minutes there was still no sign of the cougar.

"I don't think we should delay a moment longer," Miss Pringle said firmly. "As a matter of fact a thought struck me a few moments ago . . . which might well be the reason why this animal has not come for the meat."

"Yes?"

"The wind," Miss Pringle explained. "It happens

A.B.   E.

to be blowing *down* the valley. If it had been blowing from us up the valley . . . across the bracken I'm sure it would have carried the scent of meat at once to . . . er . . . Felix, if he is still here. But blowing across the bracken to us . . . I just can't see how he could get the scent."

"And . . . you will send the signal to Miss Armstrong?" There was a whole world of dejection and dismay in Avril's voice.

"I'm very sorry," Miss Pringle said, rising, "but I feel we must. After all . . . if the cougar attacks anyone we should never forgive ourselves, should we?"

Avril gulped and nodded.

Sitting with her hands clasped about her knees, she watched her companion take a white handkerchief from her pocket and begin to wave it to and fro. The French girl had keen sight, and after about a minute she thought she saw a tiny white speck appear on the rise above the unseen Brackendale farm.

"Yes, she's seen us." Miss Pringle was carrying glasses borrowed from the farm, and after waving her handkerchief had focused the glasses on the spot where Miss Armstrong should be waiting. "Well, I'm sorry, Avril, very sorry; but I am hoping now that when Ann gets our bad news she will tell her father and he will be able to stop the men coming up here with the aniseed bag. It's a great pity . . . but I don't think there was anything else we could have done, do you?"

Avril could only shake her head mournfully, and stare at the bracken. She had a feeling that Felix was in that mass of gently waving fronds; but where, she had no idea. He could not be near enough to smell the meat, or he would have come over to investigate.

They sat in silence for another twenty minutes, each busy with her thoughts. Avril could not get a picture of Bill out of her mind. There had been something very likeable about him from the very first, and the thought that they were letting him down, at a time when he was helpless, knocked the bottom out of the French girl's world.

Miss Pringle was rather relieved that the cougar had not taken the meat. When she had thought of putting aspirins in as a sleeping dose, the idea had seemed like an inspiration, a brainwave of which anyone might be proud. Once the score of little white tablets had been buried in a cut made in the meat she had started to worry. Suppose it drugged the animal so much that it died?

Suddenly both Avril and Miss Pringle were jerked out of their reveries by the sound of a voice. The speaker was not close by, but in the brooding silence of the valley the words came across quite distinctly:

"Straight up by here, Charlie," the voice said. "If we walk side by side that'll break a path through the bracken . . . so hounds can get scent an' not be held up too much."

"The aniseed men," Miss Pringle gasped, "I . . . Oooh!" Avril gave the same kind of "Oooh!" at exactly the same moment, for both had been sitting side by side and both had started to rise together.

Unfortunately Miss Pringle swung left and Avril swung right, with the result that their heads met with a real crack.

They both saw stars and recoiled to sit side by side, hands going up to eyes while heads rang with the momentary dizziness induced.

"I'm . . . sorry," Avril gasped, knuckling tears from her eyes.

"My fault, too," Miss Pringle was also at the gasping stage, for her eyes were swimming with tears while her head felt as if it had got in the way of a heavy hammer. It took them a minute or so to get over the initial shock, and when they cautiously got to their feet, the owner of the voice was only just visible more than a hundred yards away. With him was a second man, and they were speeding through the bracken at a very fast walking pace.

"Could you . . . oh, dear, I'm afraid I'll have to sit down again," Miss Pringle murmured, and did sit down. Avril recovering more quickly, dropped to her knees to ask anxiously:

"Has it . . . what . . . I'm so sorry. Look . . . I shall wet my handkerchief in the stream. You have gone quite pale."

"I . . . feel a little sickly," Miss Pringle admitted.

Avril soused her handkerchief in a nearby rill and with it mopped Miss Pringle's brow, in the centre of which a lump was rising, proof of the force of the impact when their heads bumped.

By the time they were both feeling better the two

men with the aniseed bag were skirting the top of the
bracken, completing the first leg of the trail.

"That was most unfortunate," Miss Pringle said,
brushing a wisp of wet hair from her forehead. "We'll
have to tell the men when they come down. I expect
they'll be annoyed at having been allowed to walk
all that way for nothing."

They waited anxiously as the two men, seen merely
as bobbing heads and shoulders, came down through
the bracken. When they were some fifty yards or so
away Miss Pringle said:

"I think I had better speak to them, Avril. You
won't mind me saying this . . . but as you are just a
girl they might think you were having a joke with
them. As I am an older person I hope they will take
what I have to say seriously."

"Yes," that was all Avril could say. She had the
same kind of feeling someone has who is in the middle
of a nightmare, when, in their dream, they see a
friend stepping into the roadway while a motor car,
or a runaway horse, is tearing towards them. In a
nightmare the sleeper cannot shout a warning. That
was just how Avril felt. In a matter of moments
Felix would be betrayed to these two husky young
men. The Hound Trails would be cancelled, and men
with guns would come up the valley. There would be
the sound of shots, and then a limp tawny figure would
be carried down to Brackendale, and probably put into
a cart, or in the back of an estate car. That would be
that. There would perhaps be a picture of the dead

cougar in the newspapers, an account of how it had been shot, and Bill Leaming would have lost his star performer.

She desperately wanted to do something, yet knew she was helpless. Miss Pringle was right. If the cougar did . . .!

A startled gasp from Miss Pringle brought poor Avril out of her little private nightmare. She looked up as Miss Pringle laid a trembling hand on her arm, and she, too, caught her breath.

The two men with the trailing aniseed bag were out of the bracken. Were, in fact, looking across in their direction, both men smiling. One lifted a hand in a cheery wave. Behind them, nose to the ground, as if he could not get enough of the smell of aniseed, was Felix.

In the sunshine there was something rather beautiful in his walk. His slim body was tawny in colour, and the muscles could be seen rippling under the close hair of his hide. His ears were laid back, his mouth was slightly open in a sort of silent snarl which drew back his lips and showed his polished white teeth. He padded along with such a smoothly silent tread that neither of the men he was trailing had any idea they were being followed, though Felix was not more than a dozen yards behind them.

Miss Pringle was completely frozen with horror. She knew she ought to shout a warning, but was afraid to do so in case it brought on the catastrophe she was afraid of. Somewhere she had read that the worst thing anyone could do when being stalked by a man-eater was to run. It excited the hunter, and made it easier for him to make his kill. She felt sure that if she shouted a warning, both men would begin to run.

The one hope of an un-armed man, she remembered, was to face the animal and look it straight in the eyes; but there must be no hint of fear. That was fatal. These, and similar thoughts chased one another helter-skelter through Miss Pringle's mind, and kept her completely tongue-tied. She wanted to do something but was afraid that a shout might trigger off the cougar into a run and a leap which would bring one of the two unsuspecting men to the ground.

Avril, too, stood like someone in a trance. She who was so usually full of chatter, and with a suggestion for anything and everything, was spellbound. She stood by Miss Pringle's side, too frightened to scream; too frightened to do anything but clutch at her companion's arm.

The two men strode by at speed. They were on a slight down-gradient and, now they had left the bracken behind, could hurry. The grass was short and smooth, the going good. The aniseed bag trailing behind them slithered and occasionally jumped a little when it met a slight unevenness in the ground; but all the time it was leaving its scent on the grass.

The cougar passed within ten yards of Miss Pringle and Avril, and barely gave them a glance. Whether it was the smell of aniseed, whether Felix was trying to pluck up courage to attack, or whether he just

wanted to be near the humans who all his life had
fed him, only he knew.

Suddenly the cougar paused. The rather triangular
shaped head swivelled round until the yellow eyes
seemed to be staring straight at Miss Pringle. The
nostrils dilated. Felix sniffed, sniffed again, standing in
a statuesque pose, one paw lifted off the ground as if
in the middle of a stride.

Then, slowly, as if not quite sure what he meant to
do, the cougar turned round; but now his eyes were
blazing. He went down into a semi-crouching position,
like a cat which sees a sparrow feeding in the gutter
and hopes to get near enough to spring without being
seen.

Avril heard Miss Pringle give a little gasp. She felt
the arm she was grasping tense, as if every muscle in
the older woman's body was being wound up for
some sudden, terrific action.

Felix, his head near the ground now, suddenly
bounded forward. Avril gave a little squeak of terror,
then had to turn and grab Miss Pringle. For the
English woman, with a little sigh, fainted. French
girl and English woman went down together, for
Avril was not in a position to keep Miss Pringle from
falling, though she did manage to check the collapse
and ease her to the grass.

The cougar swept by them, a tawny streak on whose
flanks the sun gleamed. If he knew they were there he
gave no sign at all, and only stopped his headlong rush
when he reached the ten pounds of beef which Miss

Pringle and Avril had left lying out in the open where the bracken ended and the bent-grass began.

It all happened in a matter of seconds, and so quietly that the two men with the aniseed bag heard nothing to make them turn round. With their thoughts on a long cooling drink, they hurried on, while behind them Avril crouched by the side of the white-faced Miss Pringle, and twenty yards farther up the valley a hungry cougar had his strong white teeth in the beef, and was facing down the way he had come, as if challenging anyone to rob him.

Avril watched him for about twenty seconds. Her heart was thumping at suffocating speed, but some of her terror was beginning to subside. She thought the danger was past. She watched Felix stand up, the lump of meat held firmly in his teeth. His tail was waving to and fro. She could hear the purring noise he was making. It was like small wooden cogwheels clicking together. Then, as if quite satisfied no one meant to rob him, the cougar turned into the bracken. Just within the green fronds he lay down, and began to eat.

Five or six minutes later Miss Pringle was sitting up again. Her face was pale, she was shaking a little, but she was rapidly regaining her composure. When Avril told her that Felix was just within the fringe of the bracken, and enjoying his meal, Miss Pringle closed her eyes for a moment, gulped, then made as if she would stand.

"We must do something, Avril," she urged. "It's

obvious that Ann did not get our message. She cannot
have warned the people that there is this animal in the
valley. We must get down there and stop the hounds
being released. If they come through the bracken . . .
following the aniseed trail, they will pass so close to
where Felix is eating he is sure to attack them. He will
think they are either after him, or after his meat.
Avril . . . help me up. We . . . oh, dear."

She tried to get up, but her legs felt so weak and
trembly that she had to sit down again at once.

"Perhaps *I* could go," Avril suggested. "I am feeling
all right again. If you stay here I . . ."

"No, no . . . oh, no. Don't leave me," Miss Pringle
begged. "I know I am being a coward, but I just
couldn't stay here alone, with that animal so near.
Stay a few minutes. I shall feel better soon, and then
we'll get down to the farm. Perhaps a minute or so
won't make much difference. What time is it?"

Avril looked at her watch. Time had just galloped
along. It was twenty minutes past twelve, and the
first Hound Trail was due to start at twelve-thirty.

CHAPTER VIII

DOWN AT BRACKENDALE farm Ann Birkett's worst fears were realised when a pale and panting Miss Armstrong tottered into the farmhouse with the news that up the valley the signal had been given that Felix had either not appeared or, if he had, had not eaten the meat.

"I'm so . . . dreadfully . . . sorry," Miss Armstrong panted. "It will be such a pity . . . to stop the . . . Hound Trails . . . won't it?"

Ann nodded dejectedly. She was not worrying very much about the Hound Trails. After all, there would be other days when the hounds could run, but if the farmers went out with their guns, this would be the last day for Bill Leaming's tame cougar.

"You . . . you *are* going to . . . tell them, aren't you?" Miss Armstrong faltered after a long silence. "I mean . . . it would be so . . . dreadful, wouldn't it . . . if someone was hurt? Lions are such terribly strong things."

"But this is a tame animal," Ann said pleadingly. "And it isn't a . . . a real lion. I mean it isn't an African lion. It . . . oh, yes, I suppose I must tell them. Even a mountain lion could be dangerous, if it was really hungry."

"I *am* sorry," Miss Armstrong quavered, "but I'm sure Jean wouldn't have sent her signal . . . if it had not been necessary. After all . . . she did think up the idea of the aspirins, didn't she? She really wanted to help."

"Yes," Ann nodded soberly. "Yes, I think she did want to help. Well, I suppose I'd better go out and . . ." She stopped there and went to the window to see who was arriving at the farm. A car had drawn up, and while there were plenty of cars bringing hounds and owners, as well as just spectators, they were all parking on the fringe of the Long Meadow.

"It's the man," Miss Armstrong whispered. "Oh, dear. I wonder what he'll do? If . . . hm! He still can't walk very well, can he?"

Ann said nothing. She was watching a police sergeant and Inspector Millom help Bill Leaming out of the car. They gave him two sticks, and as he hobbled towards the farmhouse door he kept one foot completely off the ground.

"Well, Miss Birkett," Inspector Millom said, lifting a hand in a friendly salute, "good morning. You see we've brought your guest back again, and I *have* apologised. He still won't tell us why he wants to stay in Brackendale, but we know he isn't the man from the crashed plane."

Bill smiled at Ann and winked. Then sank into a chair with a little sigh of relief.

"It'll take me a long time to get accustomed to walking with sticks," he said, "and in a way I ought to thank the inspector for ' arresting ' me. There is a small bone fractured in the ankle. So now I've got it in plaster."

Ann merely nodded. She was feeling worse than ever about Felix, now that Bill was back. When she told him the news it would wipe that cheery smile from his face.

The inspector refused the offer of a cup of coffee and left. Bill waited until he was sure no one else could hear, then asked:

"What about Felix? Did you manage to get some more meat to him? Where's the French girl?"

Ann swallowed a little lump which had come into her throat, and broke the news as gently as she could. It made her even more miserable as she watched the smile fade from Bill's face, the light from his eyes.

"Poor old Felix," he whispered, shaking his head. "It wouldn't be so bad if he was dangerous, but he isn't. He'll be far more frightened up there than anyone who sees him. He'll be like a lost child. He's an animal that never had to hunt for food. He'll be up there, scared of any strange noise, and if he did see a man at close quarters he would probably follow him . . . in the hope that he might be led back to me."

"But it is the hounds, Mr. Leaming," Miss Armstrong faltered. "We talked about it for hours last night, Jean and I. Suppose the dogs got his scent?"

"Yes," Bill admitted wearily. "The smell of a cougar might do something to them. They . . . here, could we keep the hounds from going through the patch of bracken? If we could do that . . ." He stopped, for Ann was shaking her head.

"They'll follow the aniseed trail," she explained, "and as that has been laid through the bracken, there we are. We . . ." She stopped as the kitchen door opened and the sound of nailed boots on the stone floor told of someone entering.

"Now then," came the voice of Thomas, "is there a cup o' coffee for an old man? I see no sense in buying that stuff the catering chap's selling when I can get better coffee here, for nowt."

For a moment no one answered. Ann had lifted her head a little, and there was a faraway look in her eyes. As Thomas, grumbling to himself, was turning to leave the kitchen again, Ann darted through to him.

"Thomas," she said urgently. "I want you to do something very important for me. It's very urgent; very important."

"Eeh . . . now then what have you been up to?" Thomas said, chuckling. "I know you've been doing something you shouldn't have when you come to old Thomas for a favour. You haven't robbed a bank, have you?"

"Thomas, if you didn't want the hounds to run through the bracken up the valley, what would you do?"

"Eeeh?" the old man's jaw dropped. "Stop hounds from . . . nay, nay, Ann, you know better than that. The fellers is out now dragging the aniseed bag, and once they're back the first lot of hounds will be off.

You just *can't* stop 'em." He felt for his pipe, sure sign that he was concerned. Then asked: "Ann . . . now what's gone wrong? I know you. Known you since you was a baby . . . and you're in trouble. Come on now, tell old Thomas, and if there's owt I can do . . . it's as good as done."

Ann hesitated for a moment. Bill's secret was now known to Miss Pringle and Miss Armstrong. If she told Thomas then five would know about the mountain lion.

"Waal, if you don't trust me," Thomas said, stuffing tobacco into his pipe, "seems like I can't do anything."

"Of course I trust you," Ann said, and sitting by the old man she poured out the story of Felix, Bill Leaming, the accident when she and Avril were trapped in the crevice; their attempts to make sure Felix would sleep through the Hound Trails, and the handkerchief signal which had given them the bad news that Felix had not taken the aspirin-loaded bait.

"You have been having a do, haven't you?" Thomas chuckled, and striking a match on the seat of his trousers, he sucked for a moment at his pipe. Then, with clouds of grey-blue smoke drifting towards the beamed ceiling of the kitchen, he said: "Now then, what can we do? It'll have to be done quick, and I don't mean go out and tell the Hound Trail officials. We don't want no shooting party going up after this Felix. Hm. I've got to think."

Ann poured him a mug of coffee, and he sat for a

few moments, thoughtfully sipping. Then, pulling a
face, he said:

"Nay, Ann, are you trying to poison me? Put me
some sugar in. They say sugar gives you energy, and
I need something if I'm going to think of a way out
of this pickle we're in."

He took two brimming spoonfuls of sugar, looked
up into Ann's troubled face, and with a grin said:

"Now, don't be looking like somebody what's found
a penny and lost a pound note. By this time you ought
to know as when Thomas gets his hand to summat,
you gets results. Matter o' fact I've got an idea now.
Take them light shoes off and get your boots on. You're
going to do some sweating; but I think we'll save yon
Felix . . . though there'll be a heck of a rumpus afterwards. Aye, there will an' all. Folks'll be talking about
this Hound Trail for long enough by the time we've
finished."

He finished his coffee in two gulps then hurried
out. Ann took her stout boots from the boot box and
was finishing lacing them when Thomas came back.
His eyes were twinkling, and one grey eyebrow was
cocked upwards; always a sign that he was pleased
with himself. He carried with him a faint smell of
aniseed and when he dumped an oilskin-covered parcel
on the floor he said:

"You'd better go out the back way, Ann, in case any
o' the hounds get a whiff o' that."

Ann sniffed and looked hard at Thomas.

"Well, Ann, don't look like I've set you a conundrum," Thomas chuckled. "You can guess what it is, can't ye? It's an aniseed bag . . . and stronger smelling than anyone ever carried before, I'll bet. The chaps put their stuff in the shed where I keeps my scythes, and I've used every drop of their aniseed. Now . . . you trail that bag across the *front* of the bracken . . . and if hounds don't leave the proper trail, my name ain't ever been Thomas."

For a moment Ann stared at him. What he was suggesting was that she should lay another trail . . . to take the hounds off the real scent just before they were due to enter the patch of bracken. It would short circuit the real trail, and keep the hounds away from where the cougar was lying.

"Thomas . . . " she began.

"Don't you go wasting no time, Ann," the old man warned. "Get up the valley, quick. Them lads what are laying the aniseed trail should be back in a few minutes. It won't be no use laying a false scent once the hounds are off. They'll race you hands down, y'know."

"Yes . . . and . . . thank you, Thomas."

"I'll need more'n thanks when the chaps get to know it were me what gave you that bag," Thomas said, his smile fading for a moment. Then, chuckling once more, he said: "Off wi' you, then . . . and I'll keep my fingers crossed."

"Tell Mr. Leaming," Ann said, making for the kitchen door. "He'll be wondering what we . . ."

"Ann . . . don't go, yet," Bill Leaming had hobbled

to the inner door, and must have heard much of what had been said. "Look . . . take this. If Felix is doped by the aspirins . . . you might be able to get him on a lead." And he held out the chain, with its strong leather collar at one end and the handle at the other. "He really is tame. I wouldn't let you go if he wasn't," he ended.

"What about me?" It was Miss Armstrong, her gaze going from Ann to Thomas and from him to Bill Leaming. "What am I going to do?"

"Stop here," Thomas ordered. "I dessay you're pretty good at walking the fells but you haven't seen our Ann when she's in a hurry. I doubts if you'll keep up wi' her; and she's got to move fast. You stay here, ma'am; it'll be best for everybody."

"Wish me luck," Ann said, and was gone.

She hurried through the outbuildings at the back of the farm, and up the rise where Miss Armstrong had kept watch. From there she could get part way up the valley without being seen by the crowds of men and women now thronging the Long Meadow. In that meadow excitement was growing, for the first trail was due to start in a matter of minutes. Once the two trail-layers arrived back, the hounds would be lined up. When the judges had checked the runners, the starter would give his signal by dropping a handkerchief. Then, to a chorus of excited yelps, the magnificent hounds would chase off up the valley, noses down to follow the scent of the aniseed.

As Thomas had said, Ann could travel quickly when

there was the need, and there had not been many
occasions when she had felt the need for speed as much
as she did now. With the oilskin-wrapped parcel under
her right arm, she trotted over the crest of the rise, and
saw at once that the two men dragging the aniseed bag
were within half a mile of the Long Meadow. They
would be reporting to the judges in a matter of six or
seven minutes.

She made a hurried calculation. There might be,
say, six minutes while the hounds were lined up and
last minute details attended to. Then they would be
off. And as Thomas had said, they would travel at
least twice, maybe three times as fast as Ann could go.

Glad that she was familiar with every step of the
way, Ann was able to avoid the darker green patches
which were boggy and the drier, stony places where
an ankle could be ricked as easy as wink. Keeping to
the short, smooth grass where walkers went up and
down the valley, she made good progress. She was
conscious of a peculiar whirring sound overhead, and
snatched a glance to the blue of the sky. A helicopter
was making its way over towards where the crashed
plane lay, on the other side of Tingle Crags. Over
there men were still searching for the missing man,
despite the fact that the police were convinced that he
had somehow got through their cordon, and was now
lying low in one of the larger cities.

The sun beat down, and the air was heavy with the
scent of ling and bracken. Somewhere a lark was
singing its heart out. A curlew called, its clear, liquid

notes sounding less melancholy than usual on this brilliant day.

Ann raced on. She was panting, and even her well-tried leg muscles were beginning to feel the strain. Unconsciously she was listening for the far-off yelping of hounds which would tell her the first event was under way. The sound came as she topped a rise and almost ran into Avril and Miss Pringle.

"Oh, Ann," Avril gasped, "we were coming to tell..."

Ann cut her short with a gasped question:

"Where did the men with the aniseed bag go into the bracken?"

"There ... across there." It was Miss Pringle who answered, and she stood and panted as Ann wheeled at once and began to race across the valley. Down the valley from near Brackendale farm came the music of hounds. They had got the " off ".

"What do you do?" Avril gasped, racing alongside Ann. "Is there something I can help with?"

Ann did not reply. She was tiring fast, now, for the run up the valley would have tested the muscles of anyone. Her eyes were glued on what looked like a break in the fringe of bracken. That, she thought, must be where the two men who had laid the trail had entered the bracken. She had got to be there before the first of the hounds.

As she drew near she began to undo the oilskin parcel she carried. The occasional yelp of a hound could be heard, and from the sounds the pack was obviously much nearer.

Ann had her parcel opened even as she reached the spot where a rough path had been made through the bracken. That was where the two men had ploughed a way through. In that path there would be the all-important scent of aniseed.

As Ann undid the last roll of oilskin the scent of aniseed was suddenly much stronger. Old Thomas had known what he was doing when he soaked that "drag", for he knew that the scent had to be so strong that it would turn the excited hounds.

As Ann dropped the bag to the ground, and unravelled the length of cord attached to it, Avril guessed what the ruse was.

"I shall take it," she said, holding out a hand. "I know where the other trail runs. I shall link the two, yes? Please, Ann, there is no time to spare. See . . . see the hounds."

Ann turned to look down the valley. The first of the hounds, a powerful, black, brown and white beauty was already within a hundred yards of them, and behind him were several others. They made a beautiful, exciting picture, with noses down, tails up; and they were coming along at an incredible speed.

"Stop them entering the bracken, Ann," Avril called, and started across the valley, dragging the reeking aniseed bag after her.

Ann was shaking with fatigue, and so breathless that she would have given anything to sink to her knees and let her labouring lungs fill themselves with air; but that first, powerful hound, was drawing rapidly nearer. She recognised him as one of the most popular hounds . . . Simon o' Caldbeck. He had won many events already this year.

Moving across to where the bruised stalks of bracken showed where the two men had started through the patch with their trailing bag of aniseed, she waited for Simon to reach her.

He never looked up as he galloped nearer, his nose was as near the sun-warmed turf as possible, and his nostrils were drawing in the scent. He might have been tied to some invisible rail so closely did he keep to the trail.

"Away . . . away, Simon," Ann called as the hound drew nearer. "Away," and she waved her arms to try to signal him over to her left, and so on to the trail Avril had laid.

"Away . . . AWAY!" Now there was added urgency in her voice, for Simon o' Caldbeck had not even looked up. From puppy days he had been trained to follow the scent of aniseed, and nothing short of a very high wall could have stopped him. Ann's heart was thumping faster than ever now. She knew these hounds, and she was wondering whether even the dripping aniseed bag Avril had trailed would prove strong enough to turn the hounds off the right trail.

"AWAY . . . AWAY . . . Simon!" she shouted, and for a fraction of a second the hound did look up; but he was following a story his keen nostrils were telling him. The still figure in front might have been a tree or a stone wall, something to leap over or go round.

As Ann started to wave her hands in a last desperate effort to distract Simon o' Caldbeck, the hound swerved, and was past her; the rustle of the bracken killing even the sound of his thumping pads as he raced on.

Now there were several hounds together and Ann hurried towards them, waving her hands and "shooing" them to her left. For a moment it seemed as if they, too, would swerve round her and hurry on into the enveloping bracken. They did swerve, but to her left, and that took them on to the stronger scent laid by Avril.

Without hesitation they took up the new trail, tails high, heads down, and Ann closed her eyes for a moment and knew a great sense of relief. With some hounds following the new trail there was every chance that the others coming on would also turn. They would have not only the aniseed scent to follow, but scent and sight of the hounds already ahead of them.

Within a minute every one of the first hounds had turned and was racing along the eastern fringe of the bracken. Ann watched them go and sighed with relief. Looking across the valley she could make out the figures of Avril and Miss Pringle. Avril had completed her "short circuit", and in a moment of inspiration had dumped the aniseed bag into the little stream, keeping it below the surface with the help of a large stone.

Ann did not move until she saw the first of the hounds reach the far fringe of the bracken. At that point they turned and headed down the valley. Then she closed her eyes for a moment and sighed again.

Apart from Simon o' Caldbeck the immediate danger of hounds getting the scent of Felix was over.

Mopping her wet face she began to walk across. The hounds were already growing less and less in size as they raced down the valley. They were going at a tremendous speed, for judged by ordinary Hound Trails this would be one of the easiest any of them had ever run. The real challenge of the proper trail had been the run round the bracken patch, for there the valley climbed fairly steeply, and would be a test not only of wind and limb, but also of scent power.

As she drew near Avril and Miss Pringle, the French girl, her face flushed with excitement, yelled:

"Ann . . . oh, Ann, that was wonerful. Felix did not even lift his head. We have saved him!"

Ann joined her friend and Miss Pringle. The latter had recovered now, and was almost as jubilant as Avril.

"He's eaten the meat, Ann, and seems almost ready to go to sleep. If he would only drop off . . . we . . . er . . . might be able to do something."

"I've got the leash," Ann said, "Mr. Leaming came back. The police are quite satisfied that he had nothing to do with the man missing from the plane."

"I'm . . . glad," Miss Pringle said promptly, then with a wry smile added: "I can see a rather embarrassing moment for me when I get back. I shall have to offer him my apologies. Obviously I was quite wrong, and . . ."

"Don't worry about that," Ann said, bringing from

the pocket of her twill jacket the lead. "He gave me this, and absolutely assured me that Felix would not harm us, especially if he had had a good meal. I . . . I suppose we ought to get nearer to him and see what happens. We'll have to try and win his confidence, won't we?"

She looked at Miss Pringle, then at Avril. Neither of them made any comment. Ann gave a little shrug as she said:

"If Felix was a dog . . . it would be easier. I'm accustomed to handling dogs. Mountain lions . . ."

"They *are* different," Avril said, nodding sagely. "In a story, I know that the heroine would go up quite bravely, stroke his head, slip the collar quietly round his neck, and that would be it, eh? People in stories are never frightened."

"Then I know I'm not in a story," Ann confessed ruefully. "I *am* frightened."

"Well . . ." and Miss Pringle coughed nervously. "As I . . . as I was responsible for Mr. Leaming being dragged away from the valley . . . I think it is my duty to take that chain, Ann. If you will back me up I'll try and fasten the collar round the creature's neck."

Quietly Ann held out the chain, its bright links shining like silver in the sunshine. Miss Pringle fingered the heavy leather collar for a moment, looked at the thick wrist-strap, then slipping her right hand through it, nodded:

"Well, the longer we put it off, the less we shall want to tackle the job," she said. "Shall we . . .?"

Her face was pale, but she moved towards the fringe of the bracken with purposeful steps. Avril looked at Ann, her eyebrows raised in surprise. Then she, too, started to walk towards the bracken.

Ann paused only to pick up a stone. She could just get her fingers round it. Its weight was about two pounds, and while she was hoping she would not have to use it, she held it ready. A shrewdly thrown piece of rock might put the cougar off if he looked as if he were going to attack Miss Pringle.

At the fringe of the bracken they halted. There was a faint track going up the valley from here. It was where the two men had come through the bracken on their way down after completing the top of their trail laying. Felix was lying in the warm greenery a foot or so to one side.

They could see him dimly as he lay there. He had eaten his meat and was now busy, like any domesticated cat, licking his paws and then wiping his ears. He was purring contentedly, and only looked up when he heard the three humans approaching. The purring in his throat ceased. He stirred, as if about to get to his feet, but as there was no move from Miss Pringle, Ann or Avril, he settled back again to complete his toilet.

"He doesn't sound like a wild animal, does he?" Avril suggested in a whisper. "I wonder if the tablets have begun to work? Do you think so, Miss Pringle?"

Miss Pringle shook her head. Much of her confidence in the aspirins had evaporated. She did not

think they could possibly have got to work yet. She
was now trying to decide whether it would be better
to wait here, in the hope that Felix would become
really drowsy and drop off to sleep, or whether she
should take her courage in both hands and attempt to
fasten the collar about his neck. The very thought of
doing that sent a little shiver of fear through her.

She looked at Ann, and was grateful when she got a
slow headshake.

"I think I should wait a few minutes," Ann whispered.
"After all . . . there is no immediate danger of him
being roused, is there? If we wait . . ." And there she
stopped.

The purring in the cougar's throat had ceased
abruptly. The paw which had been curling about the
left ear came down to earth with a little thump.
The relaxed muscles of the cougar tautened and the
head lifted. The eyes which had been half-closed were
now wide.

None of the three humans had heard anything, but
Felix had caught not only a sound, but also faint
vibrations. Something was drawing rapidly nearer.
A few moments earlier the cougar had been at peace
with the world. Now, he was once more afraid. He
was in a strange world, and the one person he trusted,
Bill, was not there to reassure him.

Now, even Miss Pringle could hear something. Ann
and Avril had caught the sounds before the older
woman. It was the faint sound of feet, the soft swish-
swish-swish of a body rushing through the bracken.

"Oh!" Ann gasped and lifted a hand to her lips. She had temporarily forgotten the one hound which had not taken the trail she had laid. Simon o' Caldbeck had followed the official trail, up to the foot of the Tingle Crags, round, and was now coming down on the final leg, hot-footing it for the Long Meadow and the pan of food his owner would be sure to have waiting for him.

Felix rose to his feet, his long tawny tail swishing from side to side and making the bracken sway. The purr had now become a low, threatening growl. The threshing of the hound coming through the bracken was louder, and suddenly Ann broke the silence with a warning shout:

"Simon . . . Simon . . . SIMON," and she started to run to one side, hoping to draw the hurrying hound off the trail, and so out of reach of the cougar. For Felix was obviously growing more frightened, and ready to defend himself against anything which looked like an enemy.

At the shout Felix whirled round, lips wrinkled back in a soundless snarl of fear and anger. He lifted his right paw to strike at anything, but the nearest living thing facing him then was Miss Pringle, and she was drawing back, her face ashen.

Then Simon o' Caldbeck came lunging out of the bracken. He was so engrossed in following the aniseed trail that not until he was almost into the cougar did he seem to realise that anything out of the ordinary was happening. Going at full stretch though he was,

the magnificent hound was still agile enough to make
a sideways leap as Felix swung a paw at him.

There was a startled yelp, and the hound went rolling
over and over. The thing Ann, Avril, and Miss Pringle
had feared had come to pass. Felix, his eyes blazing,
stared for a moment, then tensed for a leap and the
kill!

CHAPTER IX

FELIX MUST DIE

FOR SECONDS it seemed as if everything stood still. Simon o' Caldbeck lay twitching, then got groggily to his feet. Had he not already been leaping away the blow he had received would have broken his neck. There was a claw mark on his shoulder which was beginning to bleed, but the hound was otherwise unhurt. He stood swaying while Felix inched his hind-legs under him for a leap which would take him on to the hound.

Then Ann came to life. She leapt between hound and cougar. Her face was pale, but there was a commanding ring in her voice as she shrilled:

"Get back . . . back . . . back . . . Felix. Get back!"

Avril and Miss Pringle might have been statues for all the signs of life they gave. Both were tempor-arily petrified, and could only stand and stare. For what seemed an age Ann Birkett and the cougar stared each other full in the eyes. Ann felt that the glaring yellow orbs were beginning to hypnotise her. She could feel her knees beginning to weaken. She felt she was growing smaller and smaller while the tawny body, the sun shining full on it and revealing the muscles twitching on the powerful shoulders and forepaws, seemed to be growing steadily larger and larger.

The long tail twitched jerkily from side to side. There was a steady growl coming from the slightly open jaws. Then the yellow eyes blinked. The nervous twitching of the tail grew less, then ceased. The drawn back lips covered the polished white teeth, and Felix started to back away.

Simon o' Caldbeck, his head now beginning to clear, growled, and stepped forward. His legs were stiff, his head thrust forward. Like all his breed he knew no fear and would have gone in to the attack if Ann had not called him to heel with an imperious:

"Simon . . . SIMON! Down . . . down, boy, down."

The hound hesitated, grumbled complainingly in the back of his throat, then turned and began to head for the valley bottom. He rolled a little as if he had still not got back his full senses, but years of training were making him go on . . . to the end of the trail.

Ann wanted to stop him, but she dared not take her eyes off the retreating Felix, in case he changed his mind and came forward again. The cougar's tail was down, now, as if Ann's steady stare had demoralised him. He backed into the bracken; for a few moments he remained almost hidden by the first thin screen of fronds, then suddenly turned and bounded away up the gentle gradient.

"Ann . . . oh, Ann!" That was all Avril could say. Like Miss Pringle she had lost much of her colour, and had to clasp her hands tightly to keep them from shaking.

Ann just stood still. She had the feeling that if she moved she might fall to pieces. For those few vital moments she had risen far above her normal self, as most heroes and heroines do in time of supreme danger. When it is over there is a reaction which leaves the bravest shaken and unable to think or do anything for a little while.

Miss Pringle spoke, and despite her ashen cheeks her voice was strangely steady when she said:

"If I live to be a hundred I don't think I shall ever see anything so brave. Ann, you are a very wonderful, and a very courageous girl. I think if you had not stopped him, as you did, that poor hound would have been torn to pieces." She walked over and took Ann's hands in her own, saying: "And now we had better sit down. I, at least, am not accustomed to this kind of thing. If I don't sit down I think I shall fall down."

They sat down facing up the valley and for several minutes the only sounds came from the two or three rills which joined forces at this spot to make a stream. The water gurgled and babbled over the stones, as musically as ever. Insects droned about, and a gentle breeze made the bracken fronds wave a little. It was left to Avril to ask the question:

"What will happen now, Ann? This dog . . . hound, you call him . . . he will go back to his master. Then . . . what will *he* say?"

"I don't know. I just don't know," Ann said, a little

weariness in her voice. "By now they'll be wondering
why the rest of the hounds got back so soon. And the
people who own Simon will certainly be wondering
where he has got to."

"But what will they do when they see the slash on
the hound's shoulder?" Miss Pringle asked nervously.
"Do you think they'll guesss that . . ."

Ann shrugged.

"How can they?" she asked. "Who is going to
dream that there is a mountain lion loose up here?
They might think he's had a fight with a fox. Though
. . . well, I doubt that."

"I think we should go back and tell them what is up
here," Avril said, and then as two heads swung round
and two pairs of eyes gazed at her in astonishment she
went on: "Or . . . if we are not to do that, then I
think we should go on and find what Felix is doing.
You know what I think?"

Miss Pringle sniffed and sighed, then said:

"Avril, you have already told us what you think."

"There is something else I think that I have not told
you," the French girl said apologetically. "I think
that this Felix is *tame*! I think that a really wild
mountain lion would not have stopped for Ann . . . or
anyone else, as he did. He was very frightened, or
angry. Yet he stopped."

"What are you trying to say?" Ann asked.

"What I am going to say may sound silly," Avril
confessed, "because I am not perhaps brave enough
to do it myself . . . but I think that if we go up this

A.B.   F

valley now we shall find Felix is ready to have the
collar put on him."

"Then don't let me stop you from earning our
undying admiration, and Mr. Leaming's heartfelt
thanks," Miss Pringle said, and for the moment there
was the old note of acidity in her voice. She held out
the shining chain with its collar at one end and handle
grip at the other. "You didn't do anything when Ann
was facing the cougar. And I know I couldn't take
this leash to him now. I wouldn't have the nerve."

Avril gulped a little and nodded.

"I know. I too am not brave. Often I *dream* of doing
brave things, so that people will point at me when I
pass and say: ' Look, there is Avril Leresche who did
such a brave deed last week.' I would like people to
say such things about me; but . . ." and she shook her
head sadly . . . "I am just a dreamer. It is Ann who
is brave."

"Oh, that's fine," Miss Pringle said rather tartly.
"It's all very fine shouting, ' Hurrah for Ann,' but
I wouldn't like to ask her to face that animal again.
The very sight of its blazing yellow eyes makes me
go weak at the knees."

"You're not the only one," Ann insisted. "I'm still
trembling inside. I feel like a badly set jelly."

"So, we must go back, then," Avril commented.
"Well, I am ashamed of myself. I would like very much
to capture this Felix, but I know I have not the courage.
I am too frightened. Shall we go?"

They were a very silent trio as they got to their

feet and began to walk down the barely discernible
track which led down to the first of the farms, that of
the Birketts at Brackendale. Not a word was spoken
for the first half-mile. For each of them this retreat
was like signing the death warrant of Bill Leaming's
best circus performer.

Once the farmers knew that a mountain lion was
wandering in the hills they would not be satisfied until
it had been either killed or captured; and capturing
Felix seemed out of the question now that Bill Leaming
was out of action with his injured ankle.

Miss Pringle broke the silence with what sounded
like an apology:

"You see, it is essential that Felix be brought under
control. Not only from the point of view of people
like myself and my friend Joyce, but think of the
farmers who have sheep on the fells. Between us we
have fed Felix for two days, but if he isn't fed, then he's
going to get so hungry he'll kill a sheep. Once he
sees how easy it is to get meat that way . . . you can
guess the rest, can't you?"

Heavy sighs were the only answers she got from Ann
and Avril.

A few minutes later they halted, for from the top
of the last rise they could look down on the Long
Meadow and the Brackendale farm buildings. It was
neither the Long Meadow with its clutter of cars
and shooting brakes, nor yet the farm buildings which
halted them. Coming up the slope were men, half a
dozen local farmers, with sheep-dogs on the leash—

an unusual thing—and behind them an excited crowd
of Hound Trail spectators.

"They have got guns!" Avril said.

"Yes," Ann agreed. "And they've got the dogs on
the leash. That tells its own story. They're out after
Felix. If they weren't they wouldn't have the dogs
secure. Oh, I could cry."

When the foremost men got within hailing distance
they could see that Ann's father was among them,
and old Thomas, carrying the second of the farm
guns. And it was Thomas who shouted:

"Ah, now, there they are, safe and sound. I told you,
boss, they'd be all right."

As they drew nearer Ann did not like the expression
on her father's face. He was the kindest of men, but
could be stern enough when the occasion warranted it.
He looked very angry now. Jerking a thumb towards
the lower valley he said:

"I think you'd better get back to the house, Ann.
I'll speak to you later on," and would have walked past
the trio if Miss Pringle had not said:

"Excuse me, Mr. Birkett, but I think you would be
better with us coming along with you. We know
where this cougar went, and we have . . . er . . . had
some dealings with it."

"Hm! Dealings with it," Mr. Birkett said gruffly,
while the rest of the men gathered round. "What do
you mean . . . 'dealings with it'? I think . . ."

"If they know whereabouts it went they might
as well come. It will save time." The speaker was

Inspector Millom who had been hoping to see the second of the Hound Trails, and so had been on the spot when the injured Simon o' Caldbeck had come in.

"All right," Mr. Birkett said, "but keep behind me when we get near this lion, or whatever it is."

"It's a cougar," Miss Pringle was her calm, dignified self again, and her very self-possession seemed to put a check on the rising excitement among the men. "And don't get the idea that it is a ravenous man-eater, Mr. Birkett, I assure you it is not."

"I'll feel more assured, Miss Pringle, when I see it stretched out," was the grim retort. "Anything that hunts for its meat in my fell pastures is an enemy . . . I've got Herdwicks up there, with youngish lambs, and . . ."

"It won't kill, Mr. Birkett," Miss Pringle went on, quite undisturbed. "We happen to have fed it not an hour ago."

"Well, it'll die with a full stomach, then. Come on, we're wasting time," someone shouted, and after that conversation lagged. They were all walking quickly, and the going was uphill. When they reached the bracken they spread out. The half-dozen men with guns stood at the ready while the dogs were loosed. The unarmed spectators kept well to the rear.

Ann, Avril and Miss Pringle stood a few yards behind Mr. Birkett. They watched the bracken fronds wave as the dogs went in, and a deep silence seemed to fall over Brackendale valley as men waited. They would not have been surprised to hear a terrifying roar, or a scream of pain from one of the dogs to show that it had been surprised by the lurking mountain lion; but there was neither pained yelp nor angry growl above the rustle of the bracken. Eventually the dogs had gone right through the patch and were waiting on the scree at the foot of Tingle Crags.

No one risked walking through the bracken, despite the fact that the dogs had gone through. The men divided into two parties, one skirting the south side, the other the north. Avril and Miss Pringle took the north side with Ann and her father.

They walked along the edge of the scree, and above them, steeper than any ski-run, rose the long slope made up of small stones. Throughout the years boulders had broken off the rocky fell top and crashed down, later to be broken into smaller pieces by the bitter frosts of winter. It was rough stuff to climb and tiring work.

"If he's gone over Tingle Crags," Mr. Birkett said, "he'll be among the folk who are still searching the fells on that side. I think we ought to send someone to warn them." And he looked at his daughter for a moment, as if wondering if he should send her, or wait for someone to volunteer.

Before Ann could say she would go there was a babel of excited voices from the foot of the other scree, and when they looked half a dozen men were pointing. A chorus of shouts gave them the news that the cougar had been sighted on a ledge above the scree. They all stopped. The men cocked their guns, and took off the safety catches.

"Now, stand behind the guns, you other folks," Mr. Birkett ordered. "We don't want any accidents. If the beast comes down it'll be a case of shooting quick . . . probably a double barrel effort. I've never shot at a lion before. . . and I'm not taking any chances when I do."

The spectators were content enough to stay at the foot of the scree. Ann also stayed behind for a moment or so until Avril said:

"Ann . . . please forgive me for saying this . . . but I have a feeling that this Felix may be quite sleepy now. He has had a big piece of beef, and in it were the tablets. It . . ."

Ann hesitated, remembering how angry her father had seemed. Finally she nodded, saying:

"Yes, come on. It would be a pity if Dad shot him when he was too doped to do anyone any harm."

"I wouldn't, if I were you," Miss Pringle warned. "I don't think your father is any too pleased with us, Ann. Don't vex him any more."

Ann hesitated again, then shrugged.

"I suppose we might as well be hung for a sheep as for a lamb. And if we could do something right, Daddy might not be so angry. You stay here, Avril, and . . ."

"Ann!" There was dismay and despair in Avril's voice.

"Oh, all right," Ann agreed, and with a wry grin

added: "Yes, it might help if you come. If you are mixed up in it I dare say Dad won't feel like saying too much, since you are our guest."

They went up the scree, following Mr. Birkett, Thomas, and another farmer from nearer the village. There was no sign of Felix, but it was obvious from the shouting from the other side of the valley that the mountain lion was still visible to those on the far side.

The scree began to thin out a little, and above them stretched the sunlit masses of rock. Few people went there, for these slopes were too easy for the rock climbing experts, but a little too rough for the ordinary fell walker.

"From the way those idiots across the valley are shouting it looks as if he's farther along," Mr. Birkett said, "I'll go first, Thomas; and you follow behind me. Thomas, keep your safety catch on. I don't want the back of my neck blown off."

The third man was followed by Ann and Avril. He gave them a hard look, but did not say anything. Up here a thin wind was blowing, and the valley looked a long way down. The patch of bracken in which Felix had been hiding spread out like a dark carpet, cut here and there by a tiny thread which was one of the rivulets coming down off the rocks. Brackendale farm seemed miles away, its buildings like little boxes, the four cows in the paddock looking little more than brown and white dots.

Ann's father scrambled over a big boulder which

barred the way to where the cougar lay. He halted when over the top and turning, whispered:

"I can see him from here. Almost looks as if he is asleep."

Ann, who was at Thomas's heels, called up:

"Dad . . . Daddy," but there was no reply. Her father had turned again and her agitated whisper was blown away by the wind. "Thomas . . . let me pass. I must speak to Dad before he does anything."

"Nay, nay, Ann, you shouldn't be here," the old man cautioned. "I tell you, your father's in a fine old temper about this business. When he knew you and that French girl were up here . . . actually trying to catch that mountain lion, cor . . ." and Thomas shook his head as an indication of the state Mr. Birkett had been in.

"Come over, Thomas," came the faint voice of Ann's father. "It needs two guns for this job."

"I'll go," Ann said firmly, and as Thomas hesitated she went on. "You know I shoot better than you."

Thomas hesitated for a moment, then grunted.

"All right, have it your own way," then as Ann hesitated he grinned, gave her the gun and added: "Go on . . . you'll do better at the job than I would, anyway. But don't forget that the safety catch is *on* . . . remember, *on*. You can't shoot nothing till it's off."

Ann scrambled up the narrow chimney and over the top of the big chock stone which barred the way to the ledge where the mountain lion was resting. As she started to slither down the other side her father turned, opened his mouth to say something, only to gape in amazement when he saw that it was not Thomas, but his own daughter. Before he could get over the shock Ann said breathlessly:

"Listen, Dad, please. Let's try and *catch* Felix. He's just eaten ten pounds of meat . . . and it was doped. He should be sleepy, and . . . yes, look at him, he *is* sleepy. I'm sure we could get him tied up. I've got this leash, and . . ."

She stopped then, for Felix had lifted his head off his forepaws and looked in their direction. Then, as if not wishing to have his privacy intruded upon he got to his feet. He went quietly farther along the ledge, and was hidden by an out-jutting piece of rock.

"Augh, there," Ann's father said angrily. "If you hadn't come I'd have risked a shot at him, and Thomas could have backed me up. We'd have settled . . ."

"Daddy," Ann was trembling a little. It was the first time she could remember having a real argument with her father. Usually he was so good-tempered but now he was worried. "Daddy . . . Mr. Leaming insisted that Felix was quite tame, and that he would be much more frightened than anyone who tried to put this collar on him," and she held out the chain, with its strong leather collar at one end. "Let's try. Can we?"

For a moment her father had difficulty in choking back angry words. It was worry over his daughter and her French friend which had robbed him of his usual calm good-nature.

"We'll certainly go and look," he said finally. "You'll keep behind me, and if I can get a reasonable shot at him . . . *I am going to shoot him.* Now don't start arguing. If that cougar could claw a hound . . . he could claw you, and he could claw me. Now, be quiet."

Ann swallowed the lump which had come into her throat. There was no point in trying to argue with her father now. He was determined to shoot Felix, and if he got a chance he would do so. Holding the gun Thomas had given her she followed her father to the outjutting shoulder of rock, watched her father get round it, then followed.

As she was easing herself round the out-thrust rock she thought she heard her father suck in his breath, and her own heart missed a beat. She had a momentary idea that Felix was in position to leap at her father; perhaps had him backed against the rock face, where he could not lift his gun.

A moment or so later she was round the rock and relieved to see her father standing with feet apart, the gun held easily in both hands, as if there never had been any danger. When she looked past him she realised why he had sucked in his breath in that little gasp. She, too, stood transfixed at a sight she had never expected. She edged easily round the rock and reached her father's side, then stood transfixed. She had expected to see Felix, and the cougar was there, some seven or eight yards away. The cougar was squatting with his hind-quarters towards them, his head turned

towards the west. The sunshine was turning his tawny
coat into a shining garment of gold, which rippled
along the shoulders when he moved his head. But
it was not the cougar which riveted Ann's attention.

Behind him, half-hidden by the rock, was the body
of a man. He was so close to Felix that when that
animal's tail swept round the end flicked across the
man's head. He was lying face down, and at first
glance appeared to be either dead or unconscious. When
the tail flicked across him, however, a hand moved a
little as if to ward off the irritating thing.

"He's alive," Mr. Birkett whispered hoarsely. "Did
you see his hand move?"

Ann merely nodded. Speech just then was impossible.
There was a lump in her throat and the skin on her
neck was prickling with gooseflesh. She gave a little
start when Avril came up behind her, peering over her
shoulder to see what was going to happen.

At sight of the motionless figure behind Felix, Avril
gave a gasp of horror, one hand going to her mouth.
The cougar must have heard the sound, for his sleek
head swung round, not quickly but with a lazy movement as if he could hardly be bothered to look; and
knew he was quite safe from interruption.

Thomas, who was easing himself round the corner
of rock, called:

"Can you get a shot at him, boss?"

"Quiet . . . quiet," Mr. Birkett ordered, and edged
back a few inches, his gun coming up. Felix was

making a little grumbling noise, and seemed for a moment as if he might even get to his feet.

There was silence. Thomas remained quiet. He was unable to see anything of the cougar, but guessed something unexpected had cropped up. Felix relaxed and began gently licking one forepaw. He looked completely content.

Thomas quietly slid down off the chock stone and came up behind Avril. He took one peep over her shoulder and his eyes went round as saucers.

"Lawks, boss," he whispered. "That's put the cat among the pigeons for sure. Who's going to risk a shot with that chap lying there? Who is it?"

"Get back a bit," Ann's father ordered, and ushered them round the corner of rock. When they were out of sight of the cougar Mr. Birkett wiped a hand over his damp brow and muttered. "Well, we're in a nice pickle now. You ask who it is, Thomas? I don't know for certain, but I'll bet it's the fellow we've all been looking for. I haven't heard of anybody else missing in the fells. This chap is alive, so he can't have been there very long."

"Hm! He must have wandered along the top," Thomas mused, "and slipped. It's a living wonder he didn't go the whole way . . . though if he had he'd have been found."

"Aye, found! Found dead," Ann's father said grimly. "Point is . . . he's alive; and he's got to be moved down to safety. How the heck we're going to do it with the lion there I don't know."

"You do not intend to shoot him, Mr. Birkett?" Avril asked, hope coming to life in her voice.

"You've got to be certain of killing him first shot . . . a brain shot," Mr. Birkett said heavily. "What's going to happen if you don't, eh? He'll start throwing himself about . . . might even attack the chap; or knock him over the edge. I daren't risk it. It wants somebody with a high powered rifle . . . a crack shot."

Thomas scratched at his grey mop of hair.

"Now you're asking for something, boss," he commented. "There ain't nobody round here can shoot better than you. If you . . ."

"Dad," Ann said urgently, "I think I could get the cougar away. If I could lead him off the ledge you could . . ."

"Lead him off the ledge," her father said brusquely, "don't be silly, Ann. You get too near that animal and he'd either claw you, or sweep *you* off the ledge. Come on, we've got to get advice on this."

Refusing to listen to the pleas of either Ann or Avril he ushered them back to the chock stone. Other men were already climbing the scree, and among them was Inspector Millom.

Ann's father explained the situation, and the inspector at once asked for a volunteer to hurry down to the nearest village. He was to ring the Keswick police office and ask that an ambulance should be sent, together with a doctor, and a rifle.

"With a rifle," he explained, "the cougar could be killed with a single shot." He looked straight at Ann's father and said: "You've the reputation of being about the best marksman in the areas. I'll give you cover with a shotgun, in case you don't put him out first time. We . . ."

"Wait a moment," Ann's father interrupted. "I'm not thinking of myself; but if I didn't kill the brute with the first shot . . . what's going to happen to the poor chap lying up there on the ledge?"

That made the inspector rub thoughtfully at his chin.

"There is that point," he finally admitted. "But it's a chance we've got to take. The longer the man is left lying there, the more hopeless the situation becomes. If the cougar gets really hungry it might easily attack him."

"M'sieur," it was Avril. "Please listen. I tell you this mountain lion is tame. You understand . . . quite *tame*. His owner, Mr. Bill, said so."

There were grunts of derision from one or two of the men.

"He wasn't so tame when he had a go at Simon o' Caldbeck," one of the men pointed out.

"He really is tame," Ann added her voice to Avril's plea. "I'm sure we could get him down. Look . . . I've got this leash and collar. It would be terrible if someone shot Felix . . . and only wounded him so that he attacked the injured man. Besides, while we wait for the rifle to be brought from Keswick this man may die. Dad, we must do something now! Look, if you let me . . ."

"No," her father said abruptly, "I've said no and I mean no!"

There followed a short silence, then a man named Harter turned to Inspector Millom. Harter was one of the Hound Trail organisers; a big, bluff, kindly man.

"Look, Inspector, I'll have a go if somebody will back me up," he said. "I've been handling hounds all my life, good 'uns and bad 'uns. I reckon I know a fair bit about animals, and I dessay lions are not so much different from dogs. If this lion has just had a good meal, as the girls say, and if he's a cage-bred beast, maybe I can handle him. Give me the leash, miss. Who'll follow me with a gun . . . just in case?"

Ann gave him the leash, thanking the man with her eyes. There was a lump in her throat which prevented speech. Avril closed up to her and whispered:

"Ann, let us say a little prayer. I don't want anything to go wrong now."

They all moved up the scree until they were below the ledge on which Felix and the unknown man lay. Less than ten feet above them was their problem, but from that position they could see neither man nor beast.

No one spoke as Harter and the inspector moved away to climb up on to the ledge. They were lost to sight round a bulge of rock and would not be seen again until they had climbed over the big chock stone and were practically face to face with Felix.

While they waited there was no sound save the sighing of the wind. Then Harter came in sight. Because

of the rocky ledge they could see him only from the
waist up. Behind him, after a moment or so, appeared
Inspector Millom, his double-barrelled gun at the
ready.

Ann was tense as a bowstring as she watched the
big, heavily built Harter moving forward. He had
the leash, its polished steel links shining in the sun,
coiled easily in his right hand. As he moved quietly
forward he was talking to the cougar as he would have
talked to a bad-tempered dog. The watchers held their
breath. In the next few seconds they would know
whether Harter's confidence in his ability with animals
was justified.

Then, without warning, Felix appeared in sight.
Even Harter had overlooked one vital thing. Because
he was handling hounds almost every day of the week,
his clothes carried the unmistakable scent of dogs.
Felix got the scent, and it reminded him of his en-
counter less than an hour earlier with the hound,
Simon o' Caldbeck.

On his feet in an instant, Felix advanced, his eyes
blazing. Sure the cougar was going to attack, Inspector
Millom raised his gun and yelled:

"Duck!"

Harter turned and tried to duck at the same time,
forcing Inspector Millom to lift his gun. He was a
big man and the ledge was narrow. Balance gone,
Harter teetered for a moment as the up-swinging
double-barrelled gun blazed away. A moment later,
rather than fall off the ledge, Harter took a wild leap

out and down. The inspector followed him within seconds, the muzzles of his gun trailing thin plumes of grey-blue smoke.

Two dalesmen jumped to break Harter's fall, and for a minute or so after that there was complete confusion. Inspector Millom had taken a tumble, and was swearing and rubbing one arm. Harter and the men who had leapt to keep him from a nasty tumble had gone rolling a dozen yards down the scree.

Ann took the inspector's gun, and as she did so Harter got to his feet below them. Looking up he lifted a clenched fist and shook it, bawling breathlessly:

"You blundering idiot! Why you didn't blow my head off, I don't know. What did you think you were playing at, you gump? You panicked for nothing. That lion . . ."

"That lion was going to go for you," Inspector Millom shouted back, his face flushed with anger. "If you'd dropped to your knees I'd have had a clear shot at it, and . . ."

"Did you get it?" Ann's father asked.

"I don't know," Inspector Millom said disgustedly. "When I shouted ' Duck ' I could have put both barrels straight into the lion's head. He was only a matter of yards away, and quite still. Harter hasn't the sense he was born with. He swung round, I'd to step back . . . and chance a shot when I was off balance."

"If you hit him," Thomas said quietly, "you must have killed him. If you'd only winged him he'd have been making a row now. Mebbe you did finish him off.

It'd be as well if somebody had a look, wouldn't it?"

"Eh?" No one was keen at that moment to return to the ledge. A dead cougar was all right, but a wounded cougar, who might be waiting his opportunity to hit back at his tormentors was not the kind of creature any of them wanted to face.

"We'd better do something," Ann's father said. "Don't forget, there's that injured chap up there."

"I'll . . . I'll go . . ." Ann did not get further than that. Her father turned sharply and snapped:

"You'll stay here. If two men can't settle this animal I'm not letting you take more risks. If I . . .! What the . . .!" He stopped and looked up, his jaw dropping.

The babble of argument and comment died away, and all eyes were turned upwards. From the ledge, little more than a dozen feet above them, Avril Leresche was looking down, and calling to Ann. In the confusion of the past minutes she had gone up to the ledge, now she wanted the leash. When she was sure she had been heard she drew back and was lost to sight.

"She wants the leash!" Ann said, looking round for it.

No one spoke for a moment, than Harter gulped.

"That means . . . it's still alive," he said. "And that girl up there . . . alone."

CHAPTER X

FRENCH GIRL *v* AMERICAN LION

ANN'S FATHER reached for his gun. He ejected the spent cartridges and pushed two more home. He closed up the gun as Ann silently took the leash from the bruised and heavily breathing Harter.

"I must come," Ann said, when her father gave her a long hard stare. "I must!"

"I'd better come, too," Inspector Millom said. "Somebody give me a gun."

They climbed the scree to the right of where they stood and so got on to the ledge. When they reached the big chock stone over which they must climb, Avril was there, pale-faced and panting a little.

"I think it is better only Ann shall come," she urged. "Felix is upset. He growls . . . a little. If Ann . . ."

"I'm coming," Ann's father said grimly, "and before we do anything at all, Avril, listen to me. If there's trouble . . . you and Ann must jump off the ledge, the same way Mr. Harter did. They'll catch you below. If I have to fire I'm *not* going to miss. We've fiddled about with this business too much. Somebody's going to get hurt if the lion isn't settled once and for all.

Ann . . . remember, you jump if anything goes wrong. Avril . . . I am responsible for you. So . . . if Ann jumps, you jump!"

"I understand," Avril agreed, and taking the leash from Ann, turned. Ann scrambled over the chock stone, followed by her father and the police inspector. Then they moved round the outjutting rock face and were on the ledge with Felix.

The cougar was growling, and his eyes were flickering nervously. The two shots had frightened him badly; though not a single pellet had touched him. If Bill Leaming could have appeared at that moment the frightened Felix would have fawned on him like a pet dog. He wanted someone to pet him, to console him. He was frightened and lonely, and nothing would have pleased him more just then than to be back in his cage, with the iron bars to give him confidence.

Avril looked steadily at him, then said quietly:

"Felix . . . lie down. Lie down. Felix . . . lie . . . down. Lie down!"

The cougar lifted his head and stared at the French girl. The sun was shining full on Avril, and she had to screw up her eyes. Felix had his back to the sun and his eyes, wide open, yellow, seemed to hold a hypnotic power. Avril felt the eyes were staring right through her, drilling holes into her very skull. It was a frightening feeling.

The purring in the cougar's throat died away. Slowly he rose to his feet, his head drawn back almost as if he was afraid of a stroke from a whip. Ann could only stand and watch. Her heart was pounding like a drum. Over Avril's shoulder she could just see the head of Felix. His lips were drawn back in a silent snarl. He seemed to be challenging the French girl to come within reach of his claws.

Avril went nearer, with short, slow steps, talking all the time.

"Felix . . . you are a very good lion. Felix . . . you are a very good lion. Felix . . . lie down. Lie down . . . lie . . . down, that is a good boy."

She was within a yard of the cougar, and Felix was shrinking back on to his haunches. Ann had a terrible feeling that in a moment the cougar would leap forward, sweep round with one of his paws and send Avril hurtling over the edge, or reeling against the rocky wall.

Felix broke the silence with a snarl; then backed a pace. Avril followed him with Ann almost treading on her heels. The cougar retreated farther. Ann stepped over the outstretched arm of the man on the rocky floor. Felix was still going back, to where the ledge narrowed to nothing. He stopped only when to go back farther meant toppling off on to the screes below.

Like a cornered rat he crouched, as if daring Avril to come nearer.

"Don't try it," Ann warned. "If we can keep him here for a few minutes it will be enough." She wanted to look round but did not dare. She had a feeling that

Inspector Millom had followed her father on to the ledge, and had started to drag the limp body of the man to safety.

For what seemed an endless succession of minutes Avril faced the cougar. Felix kept his eyes glued on the eyes of the French girl. Then came a command from Ann's father:

"All right, start backing towards me. We've got the man away, and once you are safe we're going to shoot."

The words were like a stab to Ann's heart, yet she dare not disobey her father. She started to back, at the same time whispering to her friend:

"Avril . . . come on, start backing towards me. Avril! AVRIL!" more urgently now for the French girl was making no move at all to obey.

Ann's father called:

"Come on, Avril, there's a good girl. We've got the man away, and . . . hi, don't!"

Avril, instead of starting to retreat, had moved forward. Ann's blood seemed to freeze in her veins as she saw her friend reach the cougar and bend down almost as if to stroke it.

She remained like that for over a minute, then turned round. Now there was a look of mingled fear and triumph on her face as she said:

"Please go, Mr. Birkett . . . and you, m'sieur Inspector. I have got Felix on the leash. I think I can bring him down."

Ann's legs seemed to have turned to jelly. She

dared not take a step other than one which took her with her back to the rocky wall. From there she watched her father and Inspector Millom slowly back to the chock stone and scramble over it. She stood and watched Avril lead a quiet Felix past her. He walked as if he was nothing more than a big, pampered dog. The collar was buckled about his tawny throat. The chinking chain was quite slack, and Ann stood petrified until she had watched Avril coax Felix into scrambling over the chock stone. Then, her knees trembling, she followed them over and down on to the scree.

It was one of the strangest processions which went down the Brackendale valley a little later. In the lead six men were carrying the limp form of the man they had rescued. Still secured to his right wrist by a thin chain was a satchel, establishing the man as the one who was missing from the crashed plane. Some three hundred yards behind came Avril and Ann, behind them, trotting along as peaceful as any lamb, was Felix. On either side, a dozen yards distant, came Ann's father and Inspector Millom. Both men had their guns cocked . . . in case of trouble.

Stranger still was the scene when the big cougar was led into the farmyard. Bill Leaming, helped by Miss Armstrong, limped out and called to the cougar. For a moment it seemed as if Felix had not heard.

He had halted, and when Bill called him by name the tawny head turned very slowly as if the cougar did not really believe what his ears had heard. Then, proof of how quickly he could move, Felix broke free, the leather thong jerking out of Avril's hand with such force that she had to wear a bandage on her wrist for days afterwards.

Bill Leaming was bowled over, and Felix looked as if he meant to make a meal of his keeper and trainer. Even the inspector and Ann's father who had slowly begun to think that this animal from the circus must, after all, be tame, hurried up with their guns cocked anew.

Then they heard a choked command from Bill: "Sit, Felix . . . sit!"

The wrestling ended almost as abruptly as it had begun. The tawny body drew away and Felix sat, bolt upright, chain dangling from his neck, his eyes bright, a deep contented purring coming from his throat.

There were newspaper reporters and press photographers all over the Brackendale valley next day. Flash bulbs winked in the farmhouse so that pictures could be taken of the two girls indoors. Shots were taken of them outside in the sunshine. A B.B.C. Television unit arrived so that a televised interview could be made.

In the dining-room that evening they sat in the red light of the setting sun. The last reporter had gone, the last press photographer had taken his shots and made his notes. Behind the farm stood a circus wagon on which was a cage, and in the cage was Felix, a well-fed and quite contented cougar.

It was seven o'clock, and Miss Pringle turned her head as the hundred-year-old grandfather clock slowly chimed the hour.

"At this very moment," she said, beaming, "in millions of homes up and down the country the televisions will be switched on. Aren't you sorry we haven't got electricity here, and a TV set? All those other people will be able to see you two and hear you answering questions on how you captured Felix. It would be a wonderful thrill. I don't know why you refused to go into Keswick to watch the programme. I should have loved to have been televised."

Avril shook her head.

"I do not want any more thrills, Miss Pringle," she said. "Before . . . I have sighed to be famous. I have longed to walk down the street and have people turn round and whisper to one another: ' There goes that wonderful Miss Leresche; Miss Avril Leresche, from Paris. You remember what she did? She is a very brave girl.' I have wanted that."

"And don't you want it now?" Miss Armstrong asked. "After all, you really earned it, didn't you?"

"No, no," Avril protested. "I have had enough excitement, and thrills, for all my life now. I only want to walk along the paths and see mountains, and streams . . . just the quiet beauty which cannot make my heart go bompitty-bompitty-bomp."

"But you are coming to see Felix go through his act at the circus, aren't you?" Bill Leaming asked. "We're showing in Keswick next week."

Avril shook her head.

"No; please do not be angry. Ann and I have had plenty of thrills. It is plenty for all time. Now ... we take the dogs to look at sheep and lambs. Especially lambs ... I will always prefer lambs to mountain lions."

"Me, too," Mr. Birkett said, and dropping his hands into his pocket began to fumble for his pipe. He must have felt something else, however, for his expression changed.

"There is something wrong, Mr. Birkett?" Avril asked, noting his change of expression.

"No, I don't know that this is something wrong," was the reply as Ann's father took from his pocket a buff-coloured envelope. "I got it this morning ... but there's been that many folks knocking around, asking questions and stopping me from getting on with my work, it went clean out of my head."

"It's a telegram," Ann said, and felt a sudden stirring of excitement.

"It is!" her father agreed, and taking the slip of paper from the torn envelope re-read it to himself, a smile on his face. "Remember somebody was offering a reward of five thousand pounds for the recovery of the missing satchel of diamonds?"

"Oh!" The exclamation was chorused by Ann, Avril, Miss Pringle and Miss Armstrong.

"That's what *I* said, when I read it. Here, you read it. I reckon somebody's going to be able to afford a new frock, or summat. Maybe a holiday abroad. Now, now, don't tear it. Here, Avril . . . you can have first read."